THE WHITWORTH

THE LEGENDARY RIFLE

AUTHOR O.K. WILLIAMS
July 22, 2019
okwilliams.com

TABLE OF CONTENTS

Preface

THE WHITWORTH
The legendary rifle

In eighteen-fifty-four the famed British engineer, Sir Joseph Whitworth patented a unique rifle with a twisted hexagonal shaped bore that fired a large .45 caliber-500 grain bullet twisted to match that bore. This twisted bore imparted such a steady spin on the bullet that made it the most accurate rifle available in that era. When used with a specially designed Davidson telescopic sight, it had an unheard-of effective range of over 1,000 yards and had accomplished kills of up to a mile. And some say more.

Designed as a Big Game Hunting rifle, around a thousand of these rifles were built as a military rifle and some were sold to the Confederate States of America. The appearance of this rifle was very much the same as the 1863 Enfield Rifle-Musket, but that is where the similarity ends. The twisted bore made a tremendous difference to the accuracy of the rifle.

During the War-Between-the-States, the south purchased only a few of these rifles due to their high cost. [around $1,000] Because of that they were issued only to the Best-of-the-Best sharpshooters. Maximilian Trace was one of these.

CHAPTER ONE

B risk spring morning in Cox County Kentucky.
The date is April1866. One year after the end of the Civil War.

Maximilian Trace's disheveled appearance is anything but dapper. He is wearing a sweat stained slouch hat, a brown leather patch over his left eye, his left jaw is distorted with a bend that shouldn't be there, he is wearing dirty coat and trousers. His boots are covered with mud. However, he rides upright in the saddle. His head is held high. His one eye is constantly moving, taking in the entire surroundings, missing nothing. His demeaner belies his appearance.

Max rides his horse on a dirt road until he comes to a dirt driveway that turns off to the right, leading to a small log cabin, with a porch extending across the front of the house. This is the second time Max has been here. The first time was just reconnaissance This time is for a purpose. He rides on the road just far enough to see the cabin set back around 600 yards from the road, and there is smoke coming from the chimney.

He backs his horse until he could not be seen from the cabin, then turns around and retreats about ten yards. From there he walks the horse into the woods beside the road. He dismounts and ties the reins to a limb. The horse's saddle is equipped with two rifle scabbards. One the right side is the common scabbard of the day, fitted for a 44/40 caliber Henry, lever action repeating rifle. On the left side the other scabbard is unique. This one is made of stiff leather, and to cover the complete rifle it has a flap over the butt end of the stock, with a belt-and-buckle latch. Near the middle of the scabbard there is a smaller leather pocket with a similar, but smaller belt-and-buckle latch.

Limping, Max walks up to the left side of the horse, he removes the Whitworth rifle. Then from the pocket he takes a short Davidson Telescope Sight that he attaches to the left side of the rifle. [The side of the rifle, not the top.] He attaches the Davidson scope's rear mount to a specially made mounting hole in the rifle action. The front mount is made to be adjusted up and down to allow for elevation adjustment, compensating for varying distances. Max just tightens this to hold it secure, temporarily.

Max walks through the woods to the edge of the drive. He selects a stump sticking out of the ground. He lies down prone behind the stump in a position to use the stump as a steading rest. When he gets into position sighting with his iron sights at the door to the cabin. Then his eye moves to the telescope sight. He turns the focus ring on the scope until the door becomes clearly focused.

There are three hounds sleeping on the porch. He pulls the hammer back until it makes one click. [Half cock position] He reaches into a leather bag and produces a brass percussion cap and places it onto the nipple.

Max moves around until he is comfortable in his position and still aligned with his view of the cabin's door. He relaxes and waits.

In about ten minutes, former Union Private Sean O'Shee opens the door and steps onto the porch. Through the scope Max can see O'Shee clearly enough to insure it is him. He doesn't want to make any mistakes that could never be rectified. The dogs all get up and come to O'Shee, competing to be petted, Sean pets each one then walks to the side of the porch. He pisses off the side onto the ground.

While Sean was relieving himself, Max takes a flat stick resembling a ruler. He holds the top of the stick at Sean's head and places his thumbnail at Sean's feet. He pulls it back and looks at the index mark on the stick. He then loosens the front holding screw allowing the front of the telescope sight to move upward on a rack-and-pinion arrangement and tightens it at the same index mark his thumbnail indicated on the stick. He then thumbs the hammer back to the full-cock position.

Sean walks back to the center of the porch; the dogs still competing for his affection. He stretches, looking up the drive at the road.

Max makes a slight adjustment bringing the cross hairs squarely onto Sean's forehead. The rifle roars, bucking mightily against Max's shoulder.

We will never know if Sean saw the big 500 grain bullet coming, but it hit him in the forehead, propelling him backward to the door of the cabin.

Max watches as the dogs licked Sean's face. Sean doesn't move.

Max walks back to his horse, replaces the rifle and sight into the scabbard, mounts his horse and rides back the way he had come. There was no expression on his face of pleasure or sadness, just resignation. He thought, "That's one."

The sun is high over-head. Late morning of the same day. Max is in the edge of the woods overlooking a large field of weeds about waist high, that are light tan and dry from the winter weather. Nine hundred yards across the field is a small, one street town. He was looking at the back of the buildings on the North side of the street.

Former Pvt. Thomas R. Mosier comes through the back door of a small country store, carrying a box of trash. Mosier empties the trash into a barrel. He sets the box down and looks out across the field, stretching his back. A 500-grain hexagonal bullet hits him in the forehead.

While Max is riding his horse deeper into the woods, the town's people are running all around town until they find Mosier's body behind the store.

Later two armed men from the town are trampling through the weeds looking for indication in the weeds of where the shooter fired from. One says, "There ain't no weed trampled down at all. He must have shot from them woods."

"Oh, bullshit Bob, Tom was shot in the head. Ain't nobody could hit a man in the head from that far, it's gotta be seven or eight hundred yards."

"I don't know, Marty Garrett said the hole in Tom's head was hexagonal shaped. Said he knew of a Reb sharpshooter that shot a special rifle with a bullet that shape. Said one of them rifles killed General Sedgewick at Spotsylvania. Got him in the head from 1200 yards."

"Sounds like a fairy-tail to me."

"No. That's been in the papers. From the hole in the Generals head they said it was from a Whitworth Rifle."

Same day, late in the afternoon, the sun is getting close to setting. On another dirt road centered in a large pasture. An empty wagon is slowly making its way toward a turn. A loud gunshot echoes across the field and Deter Hulway falls backward then off the seat to the ground. The wagon stops. The mules stand still in their traces.

Max, taking his time, puts his Whitworth away and slowly rides away.

CHAPTER TWO

A day later in the mid-afternoon, a loan rider, with his horse at a trot was riding from the direction the town of Cox, Kentucky. He is a slim man wearing an inexpensive suit of that time. He was clean shaven except for a thin mustache. He seems extremely nervous, looking from side to side.

He comes to a driveway on the left side of the road. The mailbox there is lettered with, "MAJOR WINFIELD F WILCOX, ESQ. Attorney at Law."

Former Lieutenant Martin Garrett turns off the road on to the driveway, at a gallop. Ahead he sees a large two-story mansion. There is a very fat man standing in front of the veranda. Former Major Wilcox, He is fat, has long sideburns and a stupid looking beard that started just below his lower lip and extends to his upper chest. He walks out to meet the rider, recognizing him. "Good afternoon Martin. What brings you to my home at this time of the evening, and in such a huff?"

"We've got problems Major, big ones."

"What is it Martin.?"

'Have you heard about Tom Mosier, Deter Hulway, Sean O'Shee?"

"No. What about them?"

"They are all dead. Murdered."

"Good Lord. That is terrible Martin, who could have done such a thing?"

They were all shot with a Whitworth rifle. From a long way off. One of them up to Seven-hundred yards That's the rifle that Sharpshooter Max Trace used All three of them had hexagonal holes in the head."

"Yes, but Trace is dead. You told me yourself you saw Sgt. Bixbee run him through with his sword. Then, I know that Sgt. Bixbee and three others took him into the woods and buried him. I told them to hide his grave. I don't believe in ghosts Martin."

"Well who else could it be? They were all shot in the head with a hexagonal bullet."

"I'm, sure I don't know. It could any number of those rebels we had in that POW camp. I didn't make it comfortable for any of those vermin. Or maybe it's not connected in any way to the war or us."

"I don't know, but I'm getting a strong feeling it must be Trace."

"But, how could he do that if he is dead?"

"I'm not one hundred percent sure he is dead. Are you?"

Martin thinks back to a year ago. To events at Fort Cox, a small prisoner of war 'Holding-camp'. Designed to hold POWs until there were enough of them to send them north to the big camps such as: Camp Douglas or Elmira or Others.

CHAPTER THREE
Flash back to Camp Cox

Inside the barn of a farm that was commandeered to be used as a Holding POW camp. Max, a handsome man in his early twenties. He has a three-day beard, with no eye patch, but he Is wearing grey trousers and no shirt. He is sitting with a hoe handle just under his knees, his arms under the handle, and his wrists tied together in front of his shins. He had a stick in his mouth, being held by his rear teeth. [Called, bucked and gagged.] Max has a large letter 'M' branded on his forehead, blood running from his head, and his back showed whip stripes, some of them bleeding. His right thigh has signs of serious bleeding through an old and dirty bandage. He has obviously been beaten and tortured.

There are four Privates there. Fletcher, Gray, Hulway, and one big ugly mean looking man named Todd. Major Wilcox is standing off to the side talking to Lt Garrett. He walks over and jerks the stick from

Maxes mouth. "Now you God damn goober grabber, where is that Whitworth rifle?

Max mumbles something unintelligible. The Major walks over closer to hear what Max is saying.

"I ain't no Goober Grabber, them's Georgia boys. I'm from Tennessee."

"I don't give a damn where you are from, where is that rifle?"

Max mumbles. Major Wilcox moves closer. Max spits in his face. Pvt. Goe hits Max in the left side of his face with his rifle butt. He hits so hard Max falls on his right side. Hulway and Goe lift Max back to sitting position. Maxes left jaw is distorted and his left eyeball is lying on his cheek, hanging by a cord. Private Goe says, "That's for near biting my ear off and kickin' Sean in the nuts, and them other things you did."

The Major starts to leave. Goe asks, "What we goin' ta do bout his eye?"

Todd walks over saying, "I'll fix that." He pulls out his knife and cuts the cord, then stuffs the cord back into the socket with his finger. He walks close to the Major. He says in a low voice, "He is a danger to the men, Major. On my pig farm when we get a bore-hog that's real mean I calm him down by cuttin' his nuts out. That calms him down.

The Major nods, "If you think that will work, just don't kill him. I want to find that Whitworth Rifle.

Todd, O'Shee, Fletcher, Goe, Grey and Hulway went to where Max is still Bucked and gagged.

The Major starts walking toward the door. He turns and orders, "Put him back in his stall, when you are finished. We'll continue this tomorrow. Make sure he is not comfortable for the night, maybe he will be more inclined to talk in the morning."

A few minutes later Corporal Owen Cheatham walks into the Barn and sees what Todd and the other men are preparing to do. They have Max lying spread eagled on a couple of boards, looking like a crucifixion cross. His wrists are tied to one board going under his shoulders, and his head is tied to the other board, running the length of his spine. His trousers are off and his leg spread with two men pulling his ankles in opposite directions, exposing his genitals. "Stop this. You can't do this to a POW. It's against the rules of war. This would be called a war crime, untie him and put him in that stall where we're keeping him."

Todd got up and shoved Owen back. you stay out of this Owen. The Major said do it, and ah'm going to do it."

Owen Cheatham pushed his way between Max and Todd. Todd hit Owen in the mouth with his fist, knocking him down. Owen got back up and Todd hit him again. Todd yelled at O'Shee and Fletcher to grab Owen's arms and drag him over to a post. Todd pulled Owen's hands behind the post and tied his wrists.

Todd knelt between Max's legs and with a few deft cuts he came up with Max's testicles in his hands. He was laughing. and threw the testicles into the corner of the barn.

The next morning, April 11, 1865, at Roll Call a Colonel with an eight-man escort came riding through the make-shift gates to the camp. The Colonel rode up to Major Wilcox. "Major, the war is over. General Robert E. Lee has surrendered to General U. S. Grant two days ago, at the Appomattox Court house. Here are your orders to parole all the prisoners, close-down this camp and send them home Immediately. I will be riding by here again this afternoon. I expect it to be done." He turned and rode out amid the cheering of all the Union soldiers. The Confederate Soldiers stood around apprehensive, not sure what to expect from Major Cox.

Major Cox called Sgt Bixbee aside. Sargent, we are going to have to execute that murdering sharpshooter. He would have been brought up on war crimes and executed anyway, but we don't have time for that now, so we need to keep him from running around telling people we tortured him bringing problems and disgrace on all of us."

"You mean you and Todd, don't you?"

"Well there were many people involved in what happened to Trace, but he brought it upon himself.

"Take the men that were involved in that cutting incident. After the execution, take him out and bury him in the woods and obscure his grave so he won't be found."

16

Sargent Bixbee gathers Privates, Todd, Goe, Grey, Fletcher, and Hulway. They follow him into the barn. Sargent Bixbee walks directly to Max, draws his sword and thrusts it threw Max's stomach just below his breastbone.

They put his body into a wagon. Sgt. Bixbee and Todd were on the wagon seat, the rest are in wagon bed with the body, digging tools and a rake. They drive to a mile or so from the Camp Cox gates then turn off into the woods.

They dig a grave in the woods. It is not very deep, but they dump Max's body into the grave face down, because Hulway said that would make him go to Hell. After filling the grave with dirt, they spread the dirt out, rake it smooth and spread leaves on it, to hide the grave.

Hulway's idea about burying Max face down serves to in advertently save his life. As the working party is leaving the grave site, inside the grave Max is regaining consciousness. Max can barely breath. He panics and forces himself to push up with all the strength he can muster. This serves to give him just an inch or two, but it allows a small breathing space. He lay there regaining his strength until he can make another thrust upward. The fact that they had only buried him four or five inches allows each thrust he serves to give him just a little more breathing room.

Max was getting weaker and each thrust was less effective. He heard some voices. He did not know who they were or how far they were, but he felt he had to try to get their attention. He musters all his strength and screams for help!

One of the men hears something. He tells everyone to be quiet for a minute. The men stand there listening. There comes another fainter scream. One man says, "Somebody's in them woods over yonder, he's hollering fer help."

Another man said, "This here's Yankee territory, it ain't no affaire of ours."

"We don't know who it is and if somebody needs help, we need to be helpin' him iffen we can. I'm gonna go see what it is. Ya'll wait here fer a few minutes, Iffen Ah git in trouble, it'll be up to ya'll weather ya want to help or not."

"I'll go with ya."

"Me too."

The men walk carefully into the woods, picking up limbs and branches for weapons as they went. One-man steps on some dirt that is very soft. He said, "Dirt's real soft here."

Max heard their voices. He groans as loud as he can. The men heard it. One said, "Someone's buried here and he ain't dead."

The men started digging with their make-shift weapons. When they dig him out one man says, "That's that Reb the Yankees were beating and torturing so bad at Hell's Gate. God, it shore looks like they hurt him bad."

"Well we got to take him with us and do what we can fer him."

They make a stretcher out of some branches and some of their coats they take turns carrying him. They had earlier, decided to travel all night to get as far from Hell's Gate as they could.

In the late morning the next day they happened upon a small Union Military camp. At first, they hide. Then the man that had decided to check out the cry for help said, "This here man is goin' ta die iffen we don't get him a doctor. That camp will have a field hospital. Ya'll stay here, I'll circle around and come in from the other direction. Then I'll ask them if they will help him. Iffen they take me prisoner or something, and I don't come back by noon, ya'll just sneak on off. But if they say they will help him, and Ah think they will. I'll come git him. It's the least we can do for him."

CHAPTER FOUR
BACK TO THE PRESENT.

Maybe he wasn't dead. What if he is still alive? And what if he dug out or someone dug him out of that grave. You know as well as I do; he was one tough-son-of-a-bitch. If anyone could have survived what we did to him, it would be him."

"If Bixbee's sword didn't kill him he still would have died from that other wound you men gave him."

"Then why is this fellow killing just men from Company B? and how many men from Co. B is he going to kill? I think it is Trace Major. You didn't see him after Todd castrated him. He said, 'Ah'm going to get ya'll, for what you have done to me' His one eye showed he meant it."

"No matter how much he meant it, he can't do it if he is dead."

"He was just as calm as if stating a fact that everyone knows."

"Yes, he was an obstinate and resistant man."

"You had him beaten four times and he still wouldn't tell where that rifle was.

"Yes, I dearly wanted that rifle............ To keep the God cursed thing out of another rebel sharpshooter's hands. He would just smile at me and say, "I left it."

"One time when we untied him to eat, he liked to have choked Goe to death. I would have just let him starve to death, but you said to keep him alive."

"I wanted him to tell me where that Whitworth rifle was."

"Yes, but he never did."

"Well, ride out here in the morning and we will ride to Bent Creek and check on Sargent Bixbee, Todd and…What were those other two men from Bent Creek?

Corporal Owen Cheatham and James Gray.

And what were those two from Jude's Crossing?

"Moses Fletcher and Jacob Goe.

"Yes, them of course. I most want to talk to Sgt. Bixbee about Trace's death. And if by some strange fortune it is Trace, I'm sure his top priority would be Todd. He is the one that did that thing to him. You know the one we don't speak of." Major

Cox flashed a phony smile. Well come out early in the morning. We want to get an early start."

Lt. Garrett looked up the road show fear on his face.

The Major looked at his face. "Oh, you don't want to ride that lonely road to town. What is the matter Lt. are you afraid of ghosts?

"Not dead ones, but live ones like Trace, yes."

"Well, then you may spend the night with me. I will have one of my Negras take care of your horse.

The Next morning Major Wilcox and Lt. Garrett ride into The Mort Todd Pig farm on the way to Bent Creek Kentucky.

As they ride the Major looked at Lt. Garrett wrinkles his nose and makes a face. Acknowledging the stink, Lt. Garrett nods. They ride up to the slab side cabin.

Rebecca Todd, Mort's wife comes out of the cabin. Rebecca Todd is a strikingly attractive woman despite her unkept hair and ragged clothes. She sees them but pays no attention to them.

Unknown to her or the men Max is concealed behind bushes watching them with his telescope. He surveys the men then takes a quick look at the woman. Thinking, "If it weren't for these bastards, I reckon she would be interesting to look at." Then he looked back at the men.

Rebecca turns and hollers, "Mort, MORT, They's men here."

Mort Todd comes walking out of the barn, "Ah see'um git your ass back in that house." Rebecca goes back into the house. Mort looks at the men. "Well, well what the hell do you two want?"

Major Wilcox says, "We have come here to warn you Private Todd."

"Bout what?"

"From your demeanor I must assume you have not heard about O'Shee, Mosier, and Hulway have been murdered, over in Coxville.

"Murdered, you say, do tell, by who?"

"Lt. Garrett here thinks it might be that Reb sharpshooter Max Trace."

"Oh, bullshit. I saw Bixbee stick that som-bitch good. I helped bury him. He's dead."

Lt Garrett shakes his head, "All three of those men were shot in the head, and from some long distances. One of them from over 900 yards. Think of how far that is, and all were shot with a Whitworth Rifle.

The Major asks, "How deep did you men bury that man private?"

"Well we was in a hurry, but we did hide the grave pretty well, and it was way back in the woods. Half a mile or so from Hell's Gate." He snickers. "We buried him face down. Detter said that would make him go to hell."

"Don't call it Hell's Gate, it was Fort Cox."

The Lt. looks at Todd and rolls his eyes, Todd smiled and shook his head.

"We buried him naked so there was nothin' to identify him by."

The Major repeats, "How deep did you bury him?

"Bout two foot, maybe only a foot in some places, but hell he was dead. What difference would it make?"

"Well hell, I'm beginning to think maybe he is not dead."

Garrett says, "I think we had better tell Sheriff Miller who to be looking for. He doesn't have any idea who or what he is up against."

"No! you damn fool we certainly don't want Sheriff Miller or anyone else to catch him. If he tells Sheriff Miller or anyone what we did to him, we would all be ruined. Even union men would not look upon that lightly. I intend to run for

Congress this fall. If that got out, my chances would be sorely diminished."

Todd says, "I don't give a God damn about you running for Congress, but I ain't going to sit on my ass and let some crazy man shoot me, who-ever he is. Ro-becca, git me some vittles put in a sack, ah'm going huntin'."

"We're going with Todd he knows these woods. We must find this man. I am beginning to wish you men had not done that thing to Trace."

"Us? We did It right enough, but you are the one that gave the order to do it."

Mort comes out of the house with a Spencer rifle, a box of ammunition, and a sack of food. He is followed by his wife.

He walks to where the Lt. and the Major are arguing. Major Wilcox is saying, "I did not give that as an order. Nothing more than an off-hand remark...... Made in jest, I didn't think anyone would do it"

"I was there when you said it. Sounded to me like an order. Then you watched through the farmhouse winder."

"Well, I did not mean it as an order. "

Rebecca is listening to what was being said. "What did you soldier-boys do to that feller? "

Mort glares at her, 'None of your God-damn business. Go git my coat while ah saddle ma horse. You jest tend ta your

25

business. That is, keepin' them pigs fed and watered till ah git back."

"How long will that be?

"Ah don't know. Till ah git back here ah reckon."

The three men leave, riding in the direction of Bentcreek, Kentucky. Late-morning they arrive at Bent creek riding up to the blacksmith shop and livery stable. The shop was a large barn near the middle of town with painted sign over the large double doors, GABE BIXBEE BLACKSMITH.

The three men ride to the doors in the front of the shop. Former Sargent Bixbee walks out of the shop wearing a leather apron.

Major Wilcox says, "Good morning Sargent Bixbee.

"Morning Wilcox. Just Bixbee will do. I ain't in the army no more."

"Well, you served honorably, you certainly have the right to retain that title, in honorarium."

"You here about Tom, Sean and Deter being murdered?

"Yes. I see you Have already heard."

"Seth told us about it when he come to deliver the mail this mornin'. How's that got to do with me?"

"Did Seth tell you that all three were shot in the head, some from over six hundred yards? And that the hole was a hexagonal hole?"

"Meanin'?

"Meaning we think it could be that Reb sharpshooter, Max Trace. Only a Whitworth Rifle shoots that shape bullet. If it is Trace, he will be coming for the rest of us. He vowed he would take revenge on us. So, I am reassembling Company B and we are going after him. Get your gear together, Sargent Bixbee."

"Screw you Wilcox. I ain't in your fuckin army no more. You can't give me no orders."

"Do not presume to address me in the common. That's Major Wilcox, if you please. Or at least Mister Wilcox."

"Well ah don't please. You said ah could go by the title of Sargent because Ah served honorably. Well, by rights then you got no business callin' yourself Major because your service weren't so 'Honorarium.'"

"Don't you presume to pass judgement on me."

"Ah know why you were put in charge of that piddlin' little POW 'Holding' stockade."

"You know nothing."

"It's because one of General Thomas' Aides caught you hiding behind a tree, while you sent the rest of us charging those works at Shy's Hill in Nashville."

"There was a sharpshooter firing at me; What could I do?"

"You should have been out in front leading your men. That what most officers did. That's why they are called Leaders. Hell, they would have give you a Courts Martial if your daddy wasn't a Senator. That's why they gave you command of that little unimportant Holding Camp. They figured you couldn't fuck that up too much. But you still managed. You caused me to do the one thing Ah did in that whole war that Ah am ashamed of.

"It was a job that needed to be done."

"It weren't much of a job for a Major, an then you went and got them to let you take us boys from Cox County with you to that hell hole."

Mort looks at the LT. and smirked. Lt. Garrett just shakes his head.

The Wilcox continues, "You know if it is Trace, he will be coming for you for sure. You were the one that stabbed him with your sword. Then you buried him alive as it would seem at this point. You couldn't even do that right. That is the reason we are having this problem."

28

"He's dead, I killed him and buried him, on your orders. But while we are about it, I'm going to tell you right now; I had much more respect for Trace than Ah ever had for you. He was a hell of a hand-full, but he was a man. He damn sure wasn't a coward like you."

"He is still trying to kill us. You too."

"Maybe, but Ah ain't going with you to chase no ghost. Ah wouldn't go nowheres with you in command. Or with any of ya'll. Ah had more than enough of that. Now, go on away from here and leave me be. Bixbee turned back to his work on a wheel.

Wilcox sneered, "That arrogant bastard. Serve him right if Trace does shoot him." The three men turn their horses in the direction of Jude's Crossing.

They have only traveled ten yards when a shot rang out. Former Sargent Bixbee is knocked off his feet and lay in the dirt in the barn doorway.

The three men hastily dismount and find cover, each one seeking cover from different directions. Their heads swiveling around trying to find where the shot came from. The towns people too are looking to find some indication of where the shot originated. None of them noticed the faint whiff of smoke that is filtered by the trees from deep in the woods.

Max sneaks back into the woods keeping behind a brush that obscures his view of the town, stopping periodically to peek over the brush to see if anyone has spotted him. When he reaches his horse, he is completely hidden from the town. He mounts his horse and, this time, not taking time to case his rifle he rides deeper into the forest

Major, Lt. and Todd ride back to where Bixbee is lying in the dirt. Todd dismount and checks the hole in Bixbee's head by sticking his finger in the hole and turning it. He looks at the other two men and nods his head.

Towns people came running from all over town, gathering around Bixbee.

Wilcox, standing in his stirrups gives an impromptu speech.

"Ladies and Gentlemen of Bentcreek, most of you good people know me. For those that do not, I am Winford P. Wilcox, Attorney at Law. I had the pleasure of having this man serve under me during the recent War of Rebellion. He was a fine soldier and although our duties brought us into harm's way many times, he served with loyalty and without fault.

"Sargent Bixbee was my most trusted and loyal soldier. I will not rest until I bring his murderer to justice."

Wilcox sits back down in his saddle. Lt and Todd look at each with surprise on their faces.

"We know who the perpetrator of this foul deed, was. That is why I have reenlisted some of the loyal men of my valorous Company B to capture or put him in his grave, whatever his choice. I care not which. Although it will take precious time from my campaign and fervent wish to be elected to represent you good people in the Congress of this great United States of America, which I and this noble man here, risked our live so many times to preserve for you."

Wilcox stands again in his stirrups and waves his hand to the people of Bentcreek.

"I am sure you, wise people of Bentcreek will remember the sacrifices I am making to bring this vile murderer to justice for you. And I trust you will tell your friends of my sacrifices before the fall elections.

"We must go now and hunt down this villainous murderer.

Todd rolls his eyes, Lt Garrett Shakes his head and they turn away, a look of amused disgust pass between them.

The three men ride into the yard of former Private James H Grey. James and his very pregnant wife come out of the house to greet the men. Gray's wife Jinny stops on the porch.

Wilcox explains what has happened to James and his wife.

31

James says, "It might be Trace and again it might not, but Ah cain't just up and take off now. My woman is due most any day now."

"There is safety in numbers Private Gray. If you don't go with us, you may not live to see your baby. You wouldn't want that, now would you Mrs. Grey?

Jinny shakes her head.

James says, "Ah don't know bout this. Ah don't want ta leave her at this here time. She's from Clarksville and ain't got no kin around here and Ah ain't got no women kin neither.

Todd makes a disgusted face, "Git your gun and gear. Women have been having babies long before you have been around to hold their hand. She don't need you close by for that part of it. Now, git your God-damn gun and gear, or ah'm goin' ta whup your ass

James walks to his wife and puts his arms around her, "Were headed to Owen's, Ah'll see if Mary-sue will look in on ya."

CHAPTER FIVE

The four men ride into a farmhouse driveway with a well-maintained yard and a barn off to the side of the driveway. Former Corporal Owen J. Chatham is working at a workbench just inside the back set of double doors that open at each end of the barn. Owen hears his dogs barking. He lays down his tools and picks up his double-barreled shotgun. He cocks the hammers back on both barrels and walks to the other end of the barn. On the way he checks his Colt .45 for loads. He walks out the open double doors.

He recognizes the men. He makes a face full of disgust. He relaxes the shotgun but keeps it hanging in his right hand.

"Well, I don't have to ask what you men are doing here. That Trace feller got ya'll spooked, has he?"

Wilcox answered, "Well he certainly has us concerned. He has murdered four of our noble comrades already and is likely plotting to kill the rest of us at this very moment."

"Four, you say. I heard Three."

"He just killed Bixbee not an hour ago."

"Aw fuck. Gabe was a fine man. I hate that for sure."

"As a citizen I am willing to put my life on the line, once again, to protect the rest of the citizens of this grand district.

Owen, disgusted. "Don't stump me Major, I wouldn't vote for you if you were the last yellow dog running.

"Now what brings you here? Ah reckoned ya'll would be hidin' in a hole some-where."

Mort Todd speaks. "The Major here reckons there's safety in numbers, so we're fixin ta hunt him down before he gits us. Git your gear and let's go."

"Ah ain't going nowhere. What we did to that man was wrong then and It's still wrong now. If that is Trace out there, just maybe he has a right to do what he's doin. He's just started shootin' the wrong ones. I'm washing my hands of it."

"As ah remember it you never did git your hands dirty of it. You even tried to stop me from doing it. Until ah punched you in the face and threatened to beat the shit out of you."

"That's right Mort. I should have stood up to you then, and I didn't, but this here is a different day."

"Ah can still whup your ass, Owen."

"Nooo, Mort you can't. you've been bullying me and just about everyone else in this town since we were young'uns. I'm bone weary of it. If you fuck with me anymore, I'm going to blow your head off with this here Greener." Owen raised the shotgun to point at Mort's head.

"I should have done this back in Hell's Gate but then the Major would have had me dancin' at the end of a rope, you bein' his 'step-and-fetch-it, back then. Folks around here though, they'd likely give me a metal for shootin' your big ob—noxious ass.

The Major says, "I certainly would not have allowed you to shoot one of my loyal solders, and get away with it, for doing what he was ordered to do."

Lt. Garrett says, "If I remember right, you beat him with a whip a couple of times. My guess he will kill you just as well, if you don't help us find him."

"To find that Whitworth Rifle. At least that made some sense, to keep another Reb from getting it, but I think the Major just wanted a Whitworth rifle.

"I reckon Ah'll keep my guns loaded and my eyes open."

Lt. Garrett says, "That won't do any good, Corporal, he shoots from so far away that you won't know he is even in the County, until a bullet scrambles your brain."

Mort grins, "Personally, Ah hope he blows your head off. Ah kinda wish ah could stick around and see that."

"None the less, ah ain't goin' anywhere with ya'll. I'll take my chances. At least if ah get killed, I'll be in a lot better company, than with the sorry likes of ya'll assholes.

Mort starts to get off his horse. "God-damn you Owen, I'm goin' ta……"

Owen raises his shotgun. "Come on Mort, Ah'd as leave shoot you right here and now. That way I won't have to watch my back for the rest of my life."

"Hold on there, Corporal if you shoot Private Todd, I'd still see to it you hang for it. I have a lot of influence around here and will have more soon."

"I doubt it Major, but if so, when a man gets hung, he gets to say a few last words, don't he? Well you just guess what my last words will be about."

The Major was visibly shaken. "Oh, hell, leave him alone Private Todd, He wouldn't be much help anyway, he never was worth a damn."

"James, what the hell are you riding with these three assholes for? You've got a wife about to drop a kid any day now. You should be home takin' care of Jinny."

James looks at Mort, "Well, naw. Ah'd better go with the Major. He's right about it being safer if we are together."

"As long as ya'll are together he might leave ya be, but as soon as you split up, he'll get you. That's what Sharpshooters do, they get into position and wait until the time is right. Then they kill someone."

"He can't get us all if we are together."

"Don't bet on it. He could be right over there behind them bushes with his sights on one of us right now."

The men all look around, nervously.

The Major says, "Yes we had better get moving, since you obviously are not going to be of any help."

"Good idea Major. You just keep moving for the rest of your life. Sharpshooters usually wait until a man stops moving then he shoots them."

The men start riding back toward the road. Owen returns to the workbench near the rear door of the barn, where he had been working on a harness.

Just as he started working Max appears in the rear door with a Henry repeating rifle. Owen recoiled and started reaching for his shotgun, leaning against the workbench. Max tells him, "Just act like that shotgun ain't there. Take that Colt out of your belt, with your left hand, and lay it on the bench, then step away. You got any more guns on you?"

Owen shakes his head. "So, it is you. You ain't no ghoster?"

"No."

"We all thought you was dead and buried……..I reckon you are going to kill me now?"

"No."

Owen looks at Max with surprise. "I'm proud to hear that."

Max nods knowingly. "You were the only one that tried to stop them. I'm fixin' to kill the rest of them though."

"Not all them men were bad men. War just gets men used to killing and violence. O'Shee, he was a drunk and a wife beater, and Lord knows what else. Deter was just stupid, he didn't have sense enough to know how wrong it was."

"Make your point."

"Mosier, now he was a good God fearin' man. He regretted what was done from the git-go. He told me that just after it happened. He just didn't know how to stop it. Gabe Bixbee was a fine man but being a Sargent, he thought he had to follow orders."

"A fine man that just about murdered me."

"He was ordered to do that. And that young man James Grey, He thought he had to anything an officer or Sargent told him to. He has a young wife with a kid in her belly. You kill him, you are punishing that girl and that baby."

"He helped hold me down while they did that. How could he not know that was wrong?"

"You really want to hear it?"

"Yes, tell me how a God fearin' man could do something like that to another man."

"Well, for several years officers and non-coms have been telling us to shoot, kill, maim, and hate. It draws a pretty fine line there. Would you rather be dead than………. Well, what them men did to you?"

Max, getting angry, "You just answered your own damn question. You were able to say 'Dead', but you couldn't bring yourself to say, 'castrated'. Which, then do you think is the worst? The only thing I am living for now is to git some justice."

"Is it justice you want or just revenge?"

"I don't know, and I don't give a God-damn. I just want them dead. And in some cases, I don't want it to be easy."

"Are you familiar with the Bible?"

"My Maw and Pa died when I was six. My brother and I were raised by a spinster Aunt that went to church on Sundays and preached the Bible to us all week."

"What would she say?"

"Oh, she would say, "Leave it to the Lord. But she died when I was ten, and then I was raised by my older brother, and he would say, "An eye for an eye."

"I ain't a real religious man but I have read the book now and again. You know the book quotes on that. It says, "Vengeance is mine sayeth the lord."

"Maybe I am going against the Lord, or maybe the Lord is just usin' me to take care of this job for him."

"Well, that is a way to look on it."

"Once I get done killin' them I reckon ah will just lay down and die. Ah ain't got nothen' more to live for. Then, ah'll reckon with the Lord about it."

"I know you lost an important part of your life, but isn't there some things to live for?"

"Ah cain't fuck a woman no more. Ah only done that a few times before the war, but Ah liked it." Maxe's voice starts to get angary again. "I wanted to have a normal life, like I never had when ah was young. Now ah can never have that."

Some women don't care so much about that part of marriage."

"Well, ah care about it. And besides, what woman would like to look at this face, every morning and night. Just look at me, my jaw's all lop-sided and this patch where an eye should be, and here's a pretty thing all the ladies would like." He pulls the hair off his forehead, showing the large 'M' scar on it. That Major had Fletcher and Goe do this. He said, "Now, everyone will know you are a murderer."

"I know the terrible things Major Wilcox and the rest of us did to you. The Major was a sadistic bastard. He hated all Rebs and sharpshooters most of all. Because one got him in a lot of trouble." Owen looks down shaking his head. Then looks back at Max. "If you didn't come to kill me then why are you here?"

"Ah wanted you to know that ah wasn't going to kill you, and why I'm not going to kill you."

"I didn't help castrate you, But I did beat you with a whip. Not that I'm trying to talk you into something here." Owen's mind flashes back to a night shortly after Maxe's capture in the barn of Camp Cox.

Max remembers back to the night. It was the night Goe hit him with a musket butt, breaking his jaw and knocking his eye out of its socket. Owen had been beating Max on his bare back with a whip. "That was interrogation. Ya'll were trying to find my Whitworth rifle, to keep it out of a Reb's hands. That was a tactical thing. I understand that. The castration was just pure evil."

CHAPTER SIX

The four men ride down a short driveway, just outside of Jude's Crossing, to a small home under construction with six carpenters working on the house. Todd calls out to Moses Fletcher and Jacob Goe, "Fletcher. Goe. We need to talk to you. Come on over here."

Fletcher and Goe put down their tools and approach the Major, Todd, Lt. Garrett, and James. After talking, Fletcher and Goe talk to the job foreman. There is mild argument, but fletcher and Goe collect their Tools and ride away with the four men.

They ride to Jude's Crossing where Fletcher and Goe put their tools away at their homes and revive their guns and provisions.

Max has been following the men and watching them through his telescope. When Max had assured the men were intending to join the major's group, he back tracked toward Bentcreek. After riding one stretch of the road that went very straight for about a mile and a half then made a tight turn to the left. Max rode straight off the road where it turned. He rode into the brush where he could conceal himself and have a view straight down the road for the mile and a half.

The Major and his group would be riding straight toward Max. Giving him the same as a stationary target. A sharpshooter's preference. Max sees the men starting up the straight stretch of road. He gets into position and preps his Whitworth.

The men were riding slowly. Todd says, "We need to get the fuck off'en this road and git into them woods over yonder,

The Major gasps, "Oh good Lord no. Why should we ride in the woods with all those mosquitoes and those seed ticks that are out this time of year?"

"Better tick bit than dead, Major."

"He won't attack six of us, especially while we are moving,

The Lt. says "Yes he will. Long as we are moving straight at him."

"Well, that Whitworth rifle takes about a minute and a half to reload. If he shoots one of us, he knows that we can charge him and shoot him before he can get reloaded. The most he can get is one more of us."

"Did you ever think that he many have a second rifle, a Spencer or a Henry? If he was behind some hard cover, he could kill all of us before we got to within a hundred yards."

"Well, Lt. when did Private Todd start commanding this Company?"

"Todd is right. We need to get into those woods where he would have to get up close to take a shot. He won't get that close to six of us."

Todd sneered, "And remember Wilcox, me and you are the ones he likely wants the most."

The Major was visibly shaken by that. "Why would he want me so much? I didn't have anything to do with that thing you men did to him, or the stabbing."

Lt. Garrett made a disgusted face. "You ordered them Major."

"I most certainly did not, and I am ordering you men to stop saying that I did. I made a casual suggestion... In gest, actually I didn't expect anyone to take it seriously. Then Lt. Garrett took it upon himself to give that order."

"Major, did you ever read any of that book of Army Regulations, your daddy handed you when he gave you that uniform? It states, unequivocally, that any suggestion by a superior officer will be taken an order, You Gave those orders."

"Well, I didn't mean it as an order, and he doesn't know that, even if it were true."

Todd grins, "Well, maybe I let that slip out while I was cuttin' his nuts out."

"Well, did you? Did you tell him that vile lie? Lt., you were there did anyone say that I ordered that done?"

Lt Garrett grins, "Well I just might have mentioned it when Owen was trying to stop Private Todd."

"I know for sure Ah mentioned it. I told Owen to stay out of it cause you ordered It. Just before Ah knocked him on his ass." Todd grinned. Happy to be baiting the Major.

Lt Garrett says, "I'm pretty sure I told Owen that as well. And I know it was loud enough for Trace to hear it."

"Well Lt., you had better think of a way to let Trace know that I did not say that.

"Or what, Mister Wilcox? Something you seem to forget, none of us are in the Army anymore. You're just a private citizen now. Just like the rest of us."

"You seem to forget, I am sure I am going to have to finance this expedition, so we will do things my way or I will pull out and go home."

Todd smirks, "And do what, Mister Wilcox, just go home and wait until he kills your fat ass? Well, good riddance."

The Major is furious. "I still have a lot of influence in this County, and I will have much more when I become Congressman from this district. I can make things very uncomfortable for you.

"How much chance will you have of getting elected if word gets out that you got caught hiding behind a tree at The Battle of Shy's Hill by one of General Thomas' Staff Officers. Your daddy being a Senator is the only thing that saved you from a Courts Martial."

The Major was Panicked, screaming, "There was nothing done about that. The charges were dropped."

"Yes, but it is still in the record, that charges were brought. But that's an argument for another time right now we need to get off this road before he kills one of us. I think Todd knows more about hunting and the woods than any of the rest of us, so although I'm not saying we should put him in charge, but I think we should listen to what he says."

"And Ah'm sayin' Ah'm gittin' offen this road right now. Ya'll can come with me or stay, and Ah don't give a shit which." Todd turns off the road and heads for the woods. "You just stay here Wilcox. I'll enjoy watchin' him shoot you."

Just then Goe is knocked off his horse as if hit by a freight train.

Todd jumped off his horse and looked at 'Goe's wound. "Bullet hit just over his left eye. It was a Whitworth. He's dead."

Lt Garrett says, "Get Goe on his horse and let's get into the woods." They draped Goe over his saddle and started riding toward the woods, about ten yards away. Todd leading the way.

The rest of the men follow Todd. With Major Wilcox spurring his horse up alongside of the other men keeping to the side away from the bend in the road.

The Major started yelling at the men, "There he is at the bend of the road. Charge him. Charge him. It takes a minute and a half to reload that Whitwort."

Todd answers, "Yea and that time is up right about now. Are you fixin' to lead the charge Mr. General? Or are you going to find a tree to hide behind? You want to charge him? You jest go right ahead, Ah ain't fixin' to commit suicide."

The Major's face turns red. His hand went to the pistol in his holster. There was a sharp double click close to his ear. He turns his head to look down the barrel of Lt. Garrison's pistol. "You ain't shooting any of these men Wilcox. You try that again I'll scatter your brains all over these woods."

Todd sees what has happened. He turns and runs at the Major hitting him full force in the eye. A large lump arose over his left eye, and it was bleeding.

"You som-bitch. You were going to shoot me in the back. Ah'll fix your flint. Ah'll beat you to death, you, miserable bastard." Todd kicked the Major in the side and was preparing to kick him again." Lt. Garrett stopped him.

"Don't worry, Mort. He'll never try that again. I'll shoot him if he does. "

Todd calmed down, while Wilcox was almost crying over his wounds.

James and Fletcher move to the edge of the clearing for the road. "Ah can't see nothing."

Lt Garrett says, "He's likely gone."

Todd agrees. "Yea once we got into these woods, where he can't see us, he'll skedaddle. He don't want us to sneak up close to him in the woods."

"He seems content to just pick us off one at a time. We need to come up with a better strategy. You have any ideas, Todd?"

The Major, half crying says, "What are you asking him for? He's not in command here, I am."

"Shut up Wilcox, you are not in charge of anything.

"What do you think Todd?"

"Holey shit. The Lt done growed him a pair of balls. It's about damn time, but Ah'm proud to see it.

"Well, here's what Ah been thinkin' on, Lt. We need us some dogs."

"Dogs? What kind of dogs?"

"Ah got me some blue tick hounds back at the house, that kin foller a butter-fly through the woods. We can drop Goe off on the way, then go on back to my house and I'll git my dogs. That way we can be trackin' him instead of him trackin' us."

"Sounds like a good plan. Does every one agaree?"

Everyone agreed except Major Wilcox, who said nothing and no one seem to even notice or care.

James asks, "Since we're going past Owen's, could we stop so I can see if Mary-Sue checked on Jinny. I'm worried about her."

Garrett says, "Yea, maybe if Owen knows Wilcox ain't giving the orders he might come with us. We could use his guns."

James says, "Yea, Owen's damn good with guns."

43

The five men left stopped at Goe's father's home. Moses made the condolences to Goe's family.

The men rode back toward Todd's pig farm but stopped again at Owen Cheatham's farm.

Owen's dogs alerted him that someone was riding up the driveway. He walked out of the front door with his shotgun hanging from his right arm.

Lt. Garrett says, "Two things Owen. James here wanted to see if Your wife had seen His woman, Jenn."

"His wife. They <u>are</u> married."

"Yes, his wife, sorry."

"You should be saying sorry to 'James."

"Yes. I'm sorry James. I didn't mean any disrespect."

"Yes, James. Mary-Sue drove over this morning. She tried to get Jinny to come stay with us until after the birthin', so Mary-Sue could help her and take care of her. She told me that from the way Jinny looked it ain't goin' to be long."

"Could I talk to Mary -Sue?"

"That wouldn't be such a good idea, James. Mary-Sue is all fired pissed at you for runnin' off and leaving Jinny, in her condition. Mary's just likely to take a switch to you. And Ah might just help her."

"I feel bad about that. I just didn't know what to do."

"I'll tell you what to do." Owen's voice was getting louder. "Ride over to that wagon by the barn and wait until I get rid of these ass-holes. Then you and me will hitch my pullin' horse up to it and we will go to your house and git Jinny and bring her here, so Mary-Sue can help her.

"As for that, 'Safety in numbers' bullshit, how's that working Major? How many numbers do you need to be safe? A Squad? A company? A Regiment? How many men did you have when he killed Goe? Five. How many men did you have when he killed Bixbe? Five. James, you best take care of Jenny. There ain't no safety in the numbers you are runnin' with these jerk-offs ain't no help at-tall."

James starts his horse forward. Todd grabs his horse's bridle. He heard two double clicks. He looks down to see Owen's Greener shotgun pointing at his face.

"Let go of that horse, Todd. Or Ah'll take that ugly damn head of yours off your shoulders."

"Some day after this is settled, me and you are goin' to settle this."

"I know, I'm lookin' forward to it. But after this is settled you will likely be dead. If by some act of the devil you aint, don't be fool enough to come after me with your fists, it's going to be a gunfight. And keep in mind Mort, I'm a lot better with a gun than you are. As for me ridin' with you Garrett, there ain't a chance I hell that's going to happen."

"You know he is going to kill you too. You whipped him, and he knows it, "

"No Major he's not. He told me he wasn't going to kill me."

Lt. Garrett asks, "You talked to him? When did you talk to him?"

"Oh, about ten minutes after ya'll left. He was over in those trees watchin' while we were talkin'.

"If you talked to him, why didn't you shoot him? And Why didn't he shoot you?"

"First off, he had a .44 Henry rifle pointed at my belly button Major. Then, he said he came by to tell me he was not going to kill me. He said that I was the only one that tried to stop the castration. You see, that's what this is all about. He told me, he knew that as a Sharpshooter, if he ever got captured, he would be treated badly and possibly tortured. He expected that, but the castration was way over the line. He said you took away his whole reason for living."

The Major was relieved. "Well, then he is not after me. I wasn't even there when that happened.

"I'm going home. This is not my problem. You men can solve it by yourselves. Especially after the way you have treated me." He turns his horse to leave."

45

Owen laughed. "Oh yea, he's after you most of all, you and Todd. Because you ordered it and Todd did it and seemed to enjoy it. He said he had something special in mind for you two."

"Well then I suppose I'll have to stay."

"Hell no. You quit us so you can just stay quit. You ain't fit for nothin', no how. "

"Wait a minute Todd, We're a democracy now. We'll have to take a vote on it. We have already lost Goe and now James. That's taking us down to just three men, we need to think about this. "

"Where is Goe? Ah hope he had sense enough not to ride with ya'll?

"Trace killed him."

"Damn, he wasn't the worst of ya'll, but he was involved with the castration, and he is the one that broke Trace's jaw and knocked his eye out

"I'm. Sorry to hear that Moses, I know he was your good friend." He looked at Todd and the Major, "None of this would have been happening if it hadn't been for you two bastards. It seems he is starting with the least responsible and working toward the most responsible. I hope he does have something special for you two. It's just a shame some good men have to die because of you two."

"We need to vote. If we vote the Major out, we will have only three men left.

"Major if we vote to let you stay with the group, will you follow what the group decides and not try to run things?"

Major Wilcox was in a state of panic. "Yes, yes. I'll do what-ever is voted on. I'll even cover all the expenses. I'll even reimburse you all for lost wages."

Garrett takes a vote. "Do we want him to stay or go? Todd?"

"He goes."

"Moses?"

"Goes."

"Wait, wait. I can be some help. I'll just be one of the group. I promise. Chatham, since you are friendly with him, go to him and tell

46

him, I did not give that order. I will pay you well and be forever grateful to you. When I become a congressman there are things, I can do to help you.

"No. Ah wouldn't help you if Ah could. Ah ain't about go into those woods looking for Trace. He might just misunderstand why Ah was looking for him. And Ah damn sure wouldn't do it for you. You made your bed, now you waller in it."

Todd reaches over and slaps Wilcox's horse on the rump with his reins. Getting him started up the driveway toward the road. Wilcox was complaining, pleading and threatening all the way.

Todd says, "Come on let's go git my dogs."

James arrives to the group leading Owen's horse and wagon.

The remaining three men left. When they started away Todd turned and yelled, "James, you better git on your horse and come with us. If you don't, I guarantee I won't forget it."

James yells back, "My Jinny needs me. I don't give a damn what you do to me, I'm going to her."

From the house a woman yells, "Good for you James. Hold that wagon. I'm going with ya'll." Mary-Sue comes running from the house with a basket on one arm and a rifle under the other. "Ya'll make sure you bring your guns. That Trace feller or Todd wants trouble we'll give him a big dose of it."

James, with a grin, turned to Owen, "I shore hope I'm back on her good side!"

Twenty minutes later the wagon pulls up in front of James small cabin, with Owen at the reins. Jinny comes waddling out on to the front porch.

"Well, howdy. What are ya'll doing here?"

Mary-Sue says, "You're coming to my house until you have that baby. I ain't takin' no for an answer. Owen you and James go in and get her mattress and pillows and put them in the wagon so she can lay on them, kind-a sittin' up. Jinny you come on back into the house and tell me what to git together. All the stuff for you and the baby for a couple of weeks. Don't worry too much if we miss something. James can come back and git it, if it is somethin' I don't already have. The main thing is I want to git you to my house before that young'un decides to come out of there.

Owen looks at James and laughs. "I reckon <u>this</u> <u>ain't</u> no Democracy."

"Ah don't reckon." Is James reply, with a grin.

In ten minutes-time they had the wagon full of things Jinny thought she might need. She was reclining on the mattress with a pillow under her head and Mary-Sue was sitting on the other pillow in the bed of the wagon with Jinny.

Jinny whispered, "I am so glad you came Mary-Sue. I was so scared. Thank you." Mary-Sue nodded knowingly.

Owen started off on the road to his farm, driving slowly trying to miss all the chuck holes. When they got half-way to the Cheatham farm, a bush at the side of the road moved. Max stood up behind the bush and then let it drop. He held his Henry Repeating Rifle in his hand, hanging down. "Hold up Cheatham."

Mary-Sue made a grab for her rifle. Owen reached back and held his hand over the rifle. He tells her, "It's OK Mary. If he was going to shoot us, we would already be dead. He just wants to talk. Notice, he is not even pointing his gun at us."

"What do you want Max?"

"That feller riding with you, are you James?"

"Yes sir, Ah' am."

"Are you still riding with them others tryin' to kill me?"

"No sir, Ah ain't."

"Then Ah ain't tryin' to kill you no more. That your wife In the wagon?"

"Yes sir."

"Well, ma'am, I hope you have an easy birth and a healthy baby. You folks have a good day." He turns and starts walking toward the woods at the side of the road.

James says, "Mr. Trace" Trace turns.

"Ah got somthin' Ah want to say. Ah want you to know that Ah never felt good about what we did, Ah just didn't have the gumption to buck them like Owen did. Ah ain't saying this as a lick-finger. Sorry ladies. Most of the guards at the camp admired your grit. You was a Johnny-Reb but you showed you were a man to ride the river with.

Max looked James in the eyes for a short time, then nodded and turned back to the woods.

James says. "Did you see him? He was right there, and Ah didn't see him until he stood up."

Owen nods, "That's part of being a sharpshooter. The good ones they learn to hid in plain sight. And Ah reckon he was a good one."

Jinny says, "What in the hell was that all about?"

Mary-Sue says, "I Heard enough of you men talking to know he is going around killing men from your old outfit in the Army, but why's he doing it. The war's over, almost a year now. What's he so pissed about? And why's he being nice to you, Owen?"

"It's a long story, I'll tell you on the way home. I don't think we have anything to worry about from him."

Owen drives the wagon up as close as he could to the front door to the house.

Mary-Sue says, "Hot damn. I can see why he is so angary. I would be too. That's a terrible thing to do to a man. And you fought with that big bully Todd to try to stop it? I knew I married a damn good man." She leaned over and whispered to Owen. "We'll talk some more about this tonight; In bed."

Owen puts on his happy face.

CHAPTER SEVEN

Lt. Garrett, Mort Todd, and Moses Fletcher ride to the cabin of Mort Todd.

Todd hollers, "Ro-becca, Ro-becca where the hell are you woman?"

Rebecca come walking from the woods. "I'm here."

"What the hell are you doing in them fucking woods?"

"Hector got out of his pen. Ah was back there lookin' for him."

"How the hell did he git out?"

He got out where you fixed the pen last time. I nailed some boards over it, but Ah can't find that som-bitch. You finished huntin' that feller? Or are you going to leave me here again, with all the work?"

"Shut your face, woman. You remember what you got the last time you sassed me. I'm all fired pissed at you for letting Hector git out. I told you to watch him. He's the best breed hog in the state.

"Well, damn it, if you help me git him back in his pen, I think Ah got it fixed so he won't git out again."

"Ah ain't goin' to find him. Ah got me something more important to do. You let him git out, you find him."

"Mort, you know Ah can't handle Hector. He ain't scared of me. Ah even hit him with a stick. He still wouldn't do what Ah wanted. Can't you use the dogs to git him back in the pen. Ah think it will hold him now.

50

"No. God damn it we got to find Trace before he kills us. He's trying to kill me woman.

"Well, what are you here for?"

"Ah just come home to git my dogs to track him with. If you need help with Hector, tell Jethro to git his lazy ass over here and help you or Ah'll whup him when Ah git back.

Ah don't like Jethro around when you ain't here. He's always putting his hands on me and trying to fuck me."

"Oh hell, he ain't going to fuck you, he's your brother."

"Well he damn sure tried to time and again before daddy married me off to you and every time you ain't around."

"Just do like Ah told you. Tell him if he fucks you Ah'll stomp him good. Or go find Hector your own self and chase him into that pen, but now Git in there and fix us some supper. About that man, I'll tell you when something is your business."

"Ah reckon that answers my question."

"Shut your mouth woman and do what Ah told you.

"After we eat something ya'll can stay in the barn. We'll leave in the morning. I don't want the dogs to set on a scent at night. We'd likely be runnin' all night long, and Ah don't like chasin' him at night, even with the dogs. We don't want to run up on him by accident.

Todd was looking at Rebecca to insure she was doing what he told her to do. Garrett looks at Fletcher. He shakes his head and pinches his nose. Fletcher nods. Garrett tells Todd, "I saw a place just back the road a ways where we can make camp. We don't want to intrude on your privacy."

"Suite yourself. It don't make no never-mind to me. Ya'll can come back in the morning and we'll have a good breakfast before we leave out."

The next morning Garrett and Moses come back to the pig farm just after daybreak. After breakfast they come out into the front yard and discuss the strategy for the dogs. Todd says, "We need to go to the last place we're sure Trace was, for the dogs to pick up his horse's scent. That would be where he shot Goe from at the curve of the road.

We'll hunt around until we find sign of where he tied his horse. The dogs can git the scent from that. There will be two trails. One of him coming and one of him going. We will see which way the prints are pointing, then we'll set the dogs on his horse's trail.

In the woods adjacent to the cabin Max is kneeling behind a large rock watching the men with his telescope and listening to their plan. Max is well hidden, and his horse is tied about fifteen yards with a feed bag over his nose, to keep him quiet.

The three men ride out of the pig farm, the dogs running ahead of the men. Todd whistles from time and the dogs return to him.

Back at the farm cabin Rebecca Todd sits on a bench in front of the cabin, sobbing. If she can't get Hector back into his pen Mort will beat her, and yet she is afraid of Hector. He may be a good breed bore, but he is mean and aggressive, and he knows she is afraid of him.

The Three men ride to the spot at the bend in the road where Max had made the shot that killed Goe. They found where Max had lain to make the shot. Todd and Fletcher walked around the area, searching for sign that a horse had been tethered. About fifteen yards from the spot Max had fired from they found hoof prints and where a horse had grazed. Todd brought the dogs to that spot and held their noses to the hoof prints. Soon they started sniffing around and began wanting to go in a Southerly direction

The dogs would 'open' when they were on the scent. (continuous barking telling Todd they were on the trail.) The intensity of the barking would tell him how good the scent was. "they open, but they quiet down every now and again. That means they are on a cold trail."

The dogs would sometimes almost stop barking. The men would ride to them. They would be running around in circles sniffing the ground. If they didn't find something quick Mort would ride in the direction, he thought Max would be traveling. When he found hoof-prints he would whistle, and the dogs would come to him. He would show them the prints and they would open and take off on the trail. This went on for hours.

Max heard the dogs. He knew much about hunting dogs himself, him being raised a country boy. He could tell by the way they opened that they were not on a hot trail; most likely yesterday's trail.

In the late afternoon Max notices that the dogs braying suddenly becomes much more intense. Max correctly surmises that the dogs had at some point crossed the trail he had made today. He thinks back and remembers that he had crossed yesterday's trail today. He estimates, from the sound, that the dogs are around a half mile away.

Max kicks his horse into a trot through the woods in the direction of the creek, only twenty yards to his left. When he gets to the creek he stops and ponders. He was heading South so they will likely assume he will continue South, so he decides to back track to the North He enters the creek and continues trotting, but toward the North. He picks areas in the creek he feels will be the shallowest. He knows trotting in a creek is dangerous, but he feels he needs to get as far down the creek as he can in order to evade the group. When he gets about three-quarters of a mile down the creek he starts looking for a good place to come ashore. Just then his horse stumbles forward and falls on his chest throwing Max into the water.

Max gets up and his horse gets up. He looks at the horse and his heart sunk. The horse's right front leg was sticking out at an angle. It was obviously completely broken. He must have stepped into a hole under water.

Max led the horse to the shore. The horse limping on three legs, obviously in severe pain. He led the horse slowly to a grassy area. He removed the saddle and saddlebags; he twists the horse's head causing him to lay down on his side. He removes the Henry rifle from its scabbard

Max looked at the horse. He says, "Sorry old buddy." He starts to point the rifle at the horse's head then hearing the dogs in the distance, he laid the rifle down, drew his knife and cut the horse's throat. He couldn't take a chance of the shot telling them the direction he went, bringing the men directly to him. The horse let out a squeal then lay quiet to bleed to death.

Max removes the bridle, putting it into his saddlebag. He hung the saddlebags over his right shoulder and threw the saddle over his left shoulder, holding it with his left hand. In his right hand he carried his Henry rifle.

After moving down the path beside the creek about ten yards, it become clear as new whiskey that his bad leg was not going to allow this idea to last but a very short distance.

He set his load down, dug into his saddlebag for a bandana he kept there. He walks back to his dying horse, wipes the bandana on the horse, to get the scent on it. Then he walks back to his gear and retrieves a tin of black pepper from his saddlebag. He dumps the entire contents onto the bandana, and places it on the trail. He picks up his gear and walks on down the path another ten yards until he sees a steep hill running down from a large rock. He decides this is where he would make his stand if the men insist on continuing, after what is going to happen or if his plan didn't work. This is not the way he wanted to do this, but if he does not have a choice; So-be-it.

He hides his saddlebags, then carries his saddle with the Whitworth attached, carrying his repeating rifle in his hand, to the top of the hill. As he expected, the weight of the load took its toll, on his bad leg, so he opts to leave the saddlebag hidden. If he is still alive, he will retrieve it later. After around fifteen minutes he felt rested enough, and the dogs were still going the wrong direction, so he went back down the hill and brought his saddlebags back up the hill. He lay behind the rock, watching the best he could with his telescope.

From his cover he could see to where the horse was lying. The dogs were getting louder. He feels it won't be much longer. If his plan works, they will leave and take the dogs home. If they decide to continue their pursuit, from the very good cover of the rock he should be able to kill them all. The only place they can climb the hill is right in front of the big rock, which is so steep it will provide him plenty of time.

When the men get to the creek, following the dogs, they stopped. Todd says to Fletcher, "Put them two dogs on these leashes, hold'em here. Ah'll take the other two to the other side, an see if'en he came out or stayed in the creek. Todd rode across the creek. Two of the dogs followed him. The dogs sniffed around the other bank and found nothing.

"Well, he stayed in the creek to throw the dogs off. Bad thing is we don't know if he went North or South."

Garrett says, "He was headed South, so likely that is the way he keeps going."

"Ah don't know. He's a cagey Som-bitch. He might go North just ta fuck us up. Ah reckon hits a fifty-fifty chanst, or at least a sixty-forty chanst. Ah say let's try South first for about a mile or so. Ah don't reckon he wants to stay in the water too long cause his horse can't go fast"

The men worked both sides of the banks. They had to go slow, looking for horse tracks and wet weeds, keeping the dogs on leashes sniffing all over the banks.

After a mile Todd calls to the men on other side. "Ah reckon he hood-winked us and went North. Let's go back to where he went into the creek. Ah'll meet ya'll there.

They went back to where Max went in, then headed North doing as before. After about Three quarters of a mile they find Maxes' horse almost dead. It was obvious what had happened.

Lt. Garrett says, "He ain't gone far. He's taken his saddle, Saddlebags and that heavy rifle, as well as the repeating rifle. He isn't going far with that load. He could be in those trees aiming at one of us right now."

"Yea, and the dogs can't tell us where he is. They ain't got his scent. All's they got is his horse's scent. Let's get the dogs on leashes and get into the woods, before he shoots us.

Before leaving Garrett draws his pistole and finishes the horse.

They stayed in the woods, but as close to the path as they could. Finally, Garett saw what he thought was footprints. Todd went out to the path with his dogs. The footprints were plane and recent. He sic'd the dogs on those prints and released them. The dogs started working the scent of those prints.

Todd says, "Ah ain't for sure they're his prints, but we'll know before long. Git yer guns ready."

The dogs seem to have Maxes' scent, and are following it, until they come to an old bandana lying in the path. They opened excitedly, then all started whining and sneezing continuously.

Todd goes to them. "God-damn dirty som-bitch! Rotten bastard! Ah'm gonna cut his God damn head off and shit in the hole!"

Garrett risk exposure and comes out to the path. "What the hell is wrong, Mort?

"That som-bitch peppered ma dogs. Here, smell this here rag."

Garrett sniffed the bandana and started sneezing. "You mean he did that on purpose?"

"Hell yea, he did. Them dogs won't be able to smell they asses for three to four weeks. They'll be useless. What kind of man would do that to good dogs?"

Fletcher speaks up, "Well, if them dogs are likely to git ya kilt, Ah reckon Ah would. An you probably would too."

"Shut up Moses. They ain't your dogs."

"They ain't ruined for life Mort, they'll be right as rain in a few weeks. The worst thing is now we have to go after Trace without their help. He's proved he's a Right Cagey Dodger."

Garrett says, "If we don't have the dogs, we need to fall back and find another way. What we're doing is just going to get us all killed. He could get behind cover, we could be walking into an ambush. Less than fifty yards, and with a repeating rifle. He wouldn't miss."

The men turned around and headed back toward the pig farm.

Todd says, "Worst thing is, Ah gotta go back an find Hector in them woods an git him back in his pen, and that ain't easy without dogs, He is one mean hog."

Garrett cocks his head and looks at Todd, "Then why did you send your wife into those woods after him? Ain't you worried about her?"

"Well she let him git out,"

"She said he got out where you fixed the pen, so you must not have done that right. Don't you care nothing about her. She is an exceptionally beautiful woman. You should be protecting her."

"She may be pretty but she ain't a very good fuck. Ah git better from them whores down the bottoms."

"She's still your wife. You need to protect her."

"Mind your God damn business Lieutenant. An, my wife ain't none of yours."

Garrett looks at Fletcher, they both shake their heads.

Max watches as the men ride back in the direction of Todd's pig farm. But this leaves him on foot. He decides he will need to leave his saddle hidden and try to find a horse He has money to buy another horse but by now everyone in the county would recognize his description, a man with a patch on his left eye, a disfigured jaw, and a very pronounced limp in his right leg, carrying a repeating rifle and a big rifle in a scabbard.. It wouldn't be hard for that to start bells ringing. The thought occurred to him, maybe Owen would sell him a horse, but he rejected that idea. If he did that it would make Owen an accomplice. Max didn't want to do that.

That thought also helped him decides that, although he didn't like to do it at all, he needed to leave the Whitworth as well. He has hard enough time walking long distances without extra weight. He placed the saddle, with the Whitworth, on top of a rock then covered everything with a generous amount of small cedar trees he cut with his belt knife. He knew cedar foulage would stay on the limbs for a long time. He did take his saddlebags hanging from his shoulder.

He guessed correctly that the men would be headed back to Todd's pig farm, if nothing more, to put the dogs away.

He paralleled their movement from inside the woods, but since he could not travel as fast they got way ahead of him, but to his surprise he heard their voices ahead. He creeped closer until he realized they had stopped for the night. He skirted well around them and continued all night.

At approximately three hundred yards from the cabin he sees a path leading off the road into the woods soon he comes to a clearing just to the side of the path. It was around 4:00 in the morning, so he thought he had better get some sleep.

CHAPTER EIGHT

Max woke up late the next morning to a woman's voice. "Sew-EEEEEE, pig, pig, pig."

Max looks across the clearing. He sees a large bore hog facing the woman. She held a long stick. He recognizes her from seeing her at Todd's cabin. It was Todd's wife.

She was standing there in ragged clothes with disheveled hair, but she was still a very beautiful, very desirable woman. Max was surprised that thoughts of desire for a beautiful sexy woman like Mrs. Todd, would even be in his head. Even though he could never be able to do anything about it.

The hog was staring at the woman, swaying back and forth as they do when they are preparing to attack. The woman works her way around the bore, trying to chase him toward the farm. The hog's gaze followed her around, and he moved to stay facing her, but he made no movement in that direction. He lurched at her menacingly several time, threatening to attack. She walked forward poking at him with her stick.

"Hector, God damn you, git your ass back home. Ah'll give you some good slop. Ah even got a sow, that's come in, Ah'll put in your pen with you. Just, Please git back in your pen. She was pleading with the hog.

"Go on now, git!"

The hog attacks the woman. Just as he was getting close Max stands up from behind the bush with his Henry at the ready. He has to make a snap-shot, no time to shoulder and aim. Just as he fires the woman hits the hog in the face with her stick. His bullet hits the hog in the ribs. Not a kill-shot but enough to knock the hog on his side.

The Hog gets back up, still looking at the woman. Max moves over in front of the woman, levering another round into the rifle. The Hog attacks Max. This time Max has enough time to take careful aim and shoots the animal between the eyes, just a couple feet from himself. The hog drops dead at his feet.

Rebecca backs away from the hog, sobbing.

"It alright ma'am. He's dead."

Rebecca continues to sob.

"You just have yourself a good cry ma'am. That was a close call."

Max levers another cartridge into the Henry and waits. Rebecca continues to cry.

"You can keep on cryin' if you want to, but ya don't have to worry bout that hog he ain't no danger to ya no more."

"Ah ain't cryin' for that. When my ole' man comes home and finds out his prize breedin' bore is dead he's gonna beat the shit out of me."

At first Max is puzzled, then it dawns on him who she is. "Oh yea, your husband is Mort Todd ain't he?"

"Yes, how do you know who........Oh shit. You're him ain't you?"

"Ma'am?

"You're that Max Trace feller, Goin around killin' all them men from Mort's old Army Company.

Max hesitates, "Yes ma'am."

"Are you going to kill Mort?"

"Yes. Sorry ma'am, but yes. I'm goin' to kill him for sure."

"Kill that bastard next!   Kill him before he comes home and finds Hector dead. He'll beat the hell out of me for lettin' Hector git killt."

"You mean he would actually beat you up for losein' that hog, even if your life was in danger?"

"Oh yea. That som-bitch cares a lot more for that ole hog than he does me. An that ain't no jokein' thing."

"How'd you come to marry him? Didn't you have no idee what kind of man he was when you agreed to marry with him?"

"Ah didn't have no say in it. Ma daddy just kind of sold me to Mort for a few sows and a breed bore. Ah was only fourteen and allowed Ah had to do what ma paw said or he'd whup me." She looks down wiping her eyes on her sleeve.

"Ah didn't think Mort would be so mean to me if Ah was nice to him, but that didn't show true."

Rebecca looks up directly into Maxes' eyes. "Since you are going to kill him anyway, if you could do it before he gits home, that would save me a beatin',"

"That ain't my plan. I want to save him for last. Ah want to talk to him up close. But Ah'll see to it he don't beat you.   Tell you what, have you got a shovel and an axe at the house?"

"Yes."

Ah can bury the hog in that sinkhole over yonder. That'll keep Todd from findin' out for a while. You tell him you ain't found him yet, but you'll keep lookin'. Rekcon he'd beat you for that?"

Ah don't think so. Hector has got out before. He don't go far. I think the thing Mort will be pissed about is a couple of sows needin' serviced. It'll just delay the beatin' though."

"Ah'll be around. If it comes to that Ah'll kill him early.

Max tries but is having a hard time dragging Hector.

Rebecca looks around. "Where's your horse? You ain't walking around these woods, are you?"

"He stepped in a hole yesterday. Broke his leg. Ah had to put him down."

Rebecca grabs one of Hector's legs and helps Max pull the hog to the sinkhole. Max starts gathering stuff to throw on Hector.

Rebecca starts toward the farm. She stops, "Ah'll bring you a horse. Mort's got a pullin' horse at home. He aint much but he's broke to ride."

Rebecca leaves. She comes back shortly riding a large roan horse. She brings the axe and shovel. Max starts throwing dirt from around the rim of the pit, then threw limbs on top of that.

Rebecca says, "You can keep Zeke. He ain't fast or pretty but he's lots better than walkin'."

"Ah don't want you to get in no trouble ma'am. He's liable to hurt you."

"Won't git me in no more trouble than Ah'm already in. Ah'll just tell him Zeke went missin', ah don't know what happened to him. Mort'll think you stole him."

"That'll make me a horse thief too. Oh well, they can't hang me more than once."

Rebecca looks at him. "What did them men do to you that makes you so mad at them anyway?"

"It's personal ma'am." Max flushes, embarrassed.

"It must have been something real bad. Ah heard them sayin' they don't want nobody to find out about it. Everybody knows they killed men, what could be worse than that?"

"Something Ah don't ah don't like to talk about, ma'am, but what they did killed everything Ah ever wanted in life."

"Oh my God! They castrated you, didn't they? And I'll bet Mort did it, didn't he?

"How come you didn't kill Mort first, if he was the one that did it?"

"Ah got special plans for Mort. Ah want him to see his death commin'. That's the revenge. And Ah got some questions to ask him."

"You look like they beat the hell out of you. Did they do all that to you? Ah don't think you're ugly. You're a handsome man that got damaged some. You may still be able to find a woman. A lot of men got hurt and cripled by the war."

"Yes, but that ain't what ah'm killin' them for. Ah'm killin them for Takin' my manhood."

"Takin' your manhood? Ah don't think so! From what I've seen and heard, you are a hell of a lot more man, than all them pud-pullers. You're the only man Ah know that has been nice to me without them wantin' to get my britches off. Except one. Owen Chatham was always nice to me, but he was a few years older and so et up with Mary-Sue, he couldn't even see another girl.

"Oh fuck, Owen was in that same company with them other men. Are you going to kill him too? Please don't. He's a real good man."

Maxes' face registers surprise at her language.

"Oh, don't be surprised. My momma died when ah was a young'un. Ah was raised up with four older brothers and a daddy that didn't much mind to what they said or did around me."

"No. Ah'm not going to kill Owen. He was the only one of them that tried to stop them, from what they were doin'. He even got into a fist fight with Mort about it and got hurt a little. Ah've already told Owen that Ah aint going to kill him, long as he ain't with them trying to hunt me down. He said he wouldn't and Ah trust <u>him</u>."

"They must of beat you really bad."

"It wasn't the beating that made me swear to kill them it was the other thing."

"That part about the babies, Ah know how that feels. Ah can't have no babies nether. Mort fixed that. The pleasurin' part, that's cracked up to be a lot more than it is. Ah wouldn't care if ah never had to git fucked again."

Just then they heard Mort's dogs in the distance.

"Them's Mort's dogs. He's coming home I'd best git to the house."

"Make him think you're still huntin' for Hector. Tell him you've seen some sign. And you sure have that. Go ahead. Ah'll be watchin' If he starts to hurt you Ah'll shoot him now."

She smiles and starts walking away. 'She turns and asks, "Are you going to be here tomorrow?"

"Ah can be."

"If Mort leaves ah'll bring you some cooked food in the mornin'. Is there anything else you need." She says with a grin.

That last part seemed a little flirtatious to Max, but he dismissed it, thinking.

"Well, if you have a little extra black pepper, Ah could use a little of that."

"Sure, Ah could give you a lot of pepper." She grinned.

Max thinks to himself, "Maybe she just likes to tease. But, Ah got to quit thinking like that, no matter how desirable she is, Ah'll just frustrate myself to no end."

Todd, Garrett and Fletcher ride from the road to the shack. Todd hollers, "Ro-becca, Ro-becca. Damn woman aint never around. Ro-becca!"

Rebecca comes walking from the woods. "Here Ah am.

"Well come here. Ain't you found that hog yet?"

"Ah know where he is Ah just can't get him to come home to his pen. Ah'm goin' to git some food and make a trail to his pen. Maybe he'll eat his way there. Then ah can just close the gate.

"Well, go in the house and fix us some victuals. We're tired of eatin' trail food. Fix plenty so we can take some with us in the mornin'"

"How come you brought the dogs back? Couldn't they find his trail?

They picked up the trail and was follerin' them good until that no good Som-bitch peppered them."

"Did what?"

"He left a rag covered with black pepper layin' in the scent trail. The dogs got pepper up their noses, won't be able to smell nothin for weeks."

She fakes a cough to keep the men from seeing her laughing. "You men best be careful chasen' him he sounds like he might just be smart and powerful tough feller, as well as a good shooter."

"Shut your mouth bitch. Don't you know that man is tryin' to kill me. In the morning you go git Jethro and tell him to help you.

"No. Ah don't want him here."

"You'll do like ah told you or you'll wish you did, when Ah come back and Hector ain't here.

"Jethro won't bother you he's scared of me.

"He was scared of Daddy too but that didn't stop him, none."
"You just do like you're told."

The next morning the men ride out the driveway to the road.

After the men are out of sight Rebecca runs to the shack, She checks on the stuff that she had over-cooked for the men. While the bacon and sausage are cooking she goes into the bedroom and sits at the small dresser made of two wooden boxes and a couple of boards. She had put on a worn but clean gingham dress. She is brushing her long blond hair with a once pretty brush, mirror and comb set, holding the matching hand mirror, that had a crack across the middle of it, and the bristles of the brush are uneven and falling out. She is smiling and humming to herself.

Back in the woods at the clearing where he had killed the hog. Max is sitting on a log, his Henry rifle across his lap. His face is shaven showing his misshapen jaw. His clothes are clean, and his hat has been washed of the sweat ring. Close by is Todd's pulling horse wearing Maxes' saddle and bags. He hears someone coming up. the trail toward the clearing.

Max quickly jumps behind a tree, his rifle at the ready.

Rebecca's voice says, "Mr. Trace. Mr. Trace."

Max sees Rebecca walking into the clearing, carrying a large tray, covered with a cloth. She is looking even prettier in her clean dress and her hair combed and brushed.

Max relaxes the rifle and steps out from the tree and says, "Good morning, Mrs. Todd."

"Morning Mr. Trace. Ah brought you a little dab of food."

Max stares at Rebecca in surprise.

"Is there something wrong Mr. Trace?"

"No ma-am, You just surprised me is all."

"Well, Ah did call out to you. Knowin' you might be a little skiddish about someone coming."

"It ain't that ma-am, it's just the way you look.

"The way Ah look, Mr. Trace?

"Yes ma-am…….. You're uh………. Maybe Ah shouldn't be sayin' this ma-am but you are a rare, handsome woman…… Yes ma-am, Handsome indeed…. Striking, Ah'd say. No offence meant ma-am.

Rebecca smiles at him, "None taken Mr. Trace. Thank you. No one has ever said that to me."

"Beggin' your pardon ma-am. That's hard to believe, you bein' as pretty as you are. Hasn't Mr. Todd told you how………..Never mind, that's none of my business. You bein' a married woman and all.

"Mr. Trace you saved my life, and if you do what you say you are goin' to do you will be saving me from a life of misery. Ah don't mind you say'n you think Ah'm pretty, Ah'm real flattered. And Ah don't mind it at all." She hands him the tray of food.

"Now please eat your food before it gets too cold. It's some eggs, with pig side meat, with some light cornbread. That's cool buttermilk in that mason jar.

Max sits on the log, with the tray on his lap, taking the cover off of the tray to reveal the tray pilled high with food. "Did Ah hear you say a little dab of breakfast? A've seen less food feed a whole platoon, Mrs. Todd.

"Please call me Becca, that's what may friends call me."

"Alright Becca. Then you can call me Max. My name is Maximilian, but Max is what my friends call me."

There is a small vase on the tray filled with crocus flowers.

Max asks, "Why the crocus flowers?"

"Ah just love them, so ah thought Ah'd pick some for you."

"Ah always liked them too, they are so pretty and blond, just like you. They are first flowers to bloom in the early spring. They risk the freezing winds and snow, just get a little sunlight in their lives

"Well, thank you," She smiles at him

Max begins eating the food, but he stopped for a few seconds. "He didn't hurt you last night, did he?"

Rebecca sighs, "No more than normal."

His eyes came up to look at her. Her eyes looked down. Max realizes they were talking about two different things. She changes the subject.

"So. Does, you callin' me Becca and me callin' you Max mean we are friends now?"

"Ah'd like to think that's so, but it's a little strained. Ah'm going to kill your man. My likin' you ain't goin' to change that. It's something A'h gotta do.

"Max, Ah don't <u>mind</u> you doing that."

"Well, Ah kinda got that notion, but ah thought maybe you was just scared of a beatin' and…"

"No, it's not just that. Ah <u>hate</u> that no account bastard. Ever since he killed Ma baby, Ah told you Ah couldn't have babies no more. He knocked me down and killed my baby, still in ma stomach. It left me barren."

"Why in the world would he hit a woman in that delicate condition?

"It's not just that. The Doctor said that if Ah ever got knocked up, it would kill me. And Mort won't stop pokein' me, he says it's a man's right to fuck his woman, no matter what."

"Why did he hit you?"

"It ain't pretty. It's real embarrassin' I ain't never told nobody for fear of what they would think of me. Ah couldn't tell that to a man, and Ah aint got no lady friends. Mort don't allow that."

"Well, you don't have to tell me, if it would make you uncomfortable.

"Hell, A've done told you that Ah want you to kill ma husband. What could Ah tell you that would be worst than that. But Ah feel that Ah <u>could</u> tell you."

"Maybe you feel you could talk to me like you would a woman, because ah ain't a man no more."

"No don't you say that Max. Ah don't consider you no less a man than any man Ah've known. Just because you ain't always lookin' at my tits, like most men. Ah <u>will</u> tell you but not <u>now</u>."

"Well, Ah ain't tryin' to pry into Ya'll's intimate affairs."

"Ah ain't never fucked with any man but Mort. Partly because if Mort ever found out he'd kill me, but mostly because Ah never wanted to. Ah never liked it with Mort, so Ah never thought there was much to it. Ah think Ah would like doin' it for you. If you wanted me to. Ah think Ah'd like givin' you pleasure.

"Ah'm right sorry, Becca, but Ah can't do that.

"You don't want to? A've seen you lookin' at me, now Ah don't mind it when you do it, Ah think it's flatterin'."

"Ah ain't sayin' that. Lord knows, Ah aint ain't sayin' that. A'm sayin' Ah can't. Ah'm sorry."

"No. Don't be sorry. Ah don't care nothin' about that. Ah ain't knowed you long but Ah have taken a big likin' to you. Ah would just want to do it for you, not for me.

"Well, that could never happen. Mort and them other men that helped him made that impossible. When they castrated me they took that from me. ''

"Mort did it didn't he?

"Yea and Ah think he liked it. They didn't just hurt me, they took my whole life from me. Ah wanted to get married and build something lasting for the young'uns, my wife and Ah made in our bed."

"You could still do most of that. Ah know you can't give a woman babies, but there are lots of war orphans around that need someone to raise them up."

"They wouldn't be my blood."

"No, but if you raised them up, you'd come to love them just the same and they would love you.

"Just where am Ah going to find a woman to share my life with. Ah can't pleasure her and she can't pleasure me.

"If a woman really loved a man, she wouldn't care about those things so much."

"And how am Ah going to attract a woman like that with a face as ugly as mine. She'd be ashamed to walk down the street with me. And look at this," He pulled his hair back from his forehead, showing the 'M' Scare burned on it.

You ain't ugly Max. You're a handsome man that's been damaged. Ah can see what a handsome man you really are, under that patch and what happened to your jaw, and lots of men came back from the war limpin'. Now you just think about Mort, That's, a real ugly som-bitch, and he ain't even been damaged. He's just natural ugly.

"let me see now; I'd have to find me a woman that don't mind that Ah can't give her no babies, don't mind that ah can't pleasure her, and don't mind that ah have a face that would scare young'uns on All Haints Day."

"There are women like that about."

"Well there's maybe three or four of them in this country. And likely a couple of them are in the North and wouldn't want no truck with a Southerner. So now how am Ah going to find one of the other two that's left?"

Rebecca stands up. "Right here Max. Right here in front of you."

Max was stunned. He stood there looking at one of the most desirable women he had ever known, trying to accept what he thought she was saying. "Are you sayin' that you could hitch up, and maybe even marry a man that looks like me?"

"Max Ah would much rather spend the rest of my life with a man just like you, than one more day with that miserable dammed Mort Todd.

"No that's wrong Max. I didn't mean a man like you,' Ah meant with you, Max. With YOU!"

But you are still married to Mort."

"Until death do us part."

"Becca, if your saying that to make sure Ah'm gonna kill Mort, you don't have to. Ah am going to kill him, no matter what else."

"Ah know. Thank you." Rebecca moves forward and hugs Max. They embrace for a few seconds

"Ah've got to go now Becca. Ah'll come back in a few days. Ah'm going to think on what you said. You think on it too. You would be committing yourself to a life with half a man. I won't hold you to nothin'"

"Please don't say that Max. I will never think on you as half a man. You're the best man Ah ever met. Ah don't think Ah'll change my mind.

"How will Ah know when you are back?"

"You'll know."

Rebecca says, "Be careful Max, please!" she moves in to embrace him again. This time she gives him a very passionate kiss and holds him tightly. The expression on her face is one of contented bliss, then changes to wide eyed surprise, with a slight smile. She feels him getting an erection.

CHAPTER NINE

The Cox County Sheriff and four men ride in on the driveway of the Wilcox Family Plantation. Major Wilcox walks out of the house onto the front lawn.

"Good afternoon Sheriff Barton. "

The Sheriff dismounts and walks to Wilcox. "Call your men out of the field Major. Before the rest of them get killed. That man is obviously after you and the men that were in your command. For whatever reason. You would be far better served Bringing them all here and setting up some sort of cover. This man is damn good at what he does. Your men are no match for him in the woods."

"Yes, I tried to tell them that, but they wouldn't listen. I have hired some men from out of the county to handle that task. I'm sure that Lt. Garrett and Mort Todd will find him and eliminate the danger to this county."

"Well, I don't share your optimism."

"Yes, well he was a Sharpshooter, which brings me to my advice to you. Don't get close to him. Don't try to capture him. Kill him. Even if he is wounded, he is very dangerous, do not approach him. Sorely injured and unarmed he almost killed some of my men. He is delusional. He accused them of terrible atrocities, that I know weren't true.

The Sheriff looks at Wilcox with skepticism.

"I think part of his insanity could stem from the fact that someone, long ago had castrated him. Long before he was captured and brought to Fort Cox. But in his delirium, he even accused us of that. Don't try to take him alive."

"What you are saying is you don't want us to capture him?"

"I just don't want any of your brave men to be killed or injured trying to capture a crazy man that will just spend, the rest of his life in an asylum. A fate worse than death in my opinion."

"Why am I getting the opinion there is more to this than I am being told?"

"Why, I don't know why you would think such a thing."

"Because he don't seem like a crazy man to me. He is one pissed off son-of-a-bitch, but he is very smart, very rational, and very skilled."

The next morning in the woods within sight of the Wilcox Mansion, four men are sitting around a campfire cooking their breakfast. A coffee pot is setting close to the flames and a skillet was on the fire frying some bacon.

All the men were armed with repeating rifles and handguns.

Man #1 is saying, "Old Major Wilcox would be mad as hell if he knew all of us were eating at the same time. He said to keep two of us riding and take turns eatin'. He said that Reb feller is liable to sneak up anytime.

Man #2 says, "Screw him. We got to eat, and there ain't no sense in fixin' breakfast two or three times. Wilcox acts to me like he is scared shitless of that Reb.

Man #3, "He says that feller is as dangerous as two-dollar pistole. Done killed four or five men."

Man #2, "Well, we ain't seed hid-nor-hair of him. Ah don't reckon he's anywhere here-abouts."

Man #1 "What do you reckon that Reb. Is so pissed about. Killin' all those men that were POW camp guards.?"

"Maybe they didn't feed him enough corn-pone, is what pissed him off."

The men laughed.

Man#4, "Well he's shore got the Major spooked. He said, 'Don't even try to take him alive, just kill him,' says he. He said that about ten times. When he was talkin' to us,"

Man #3, "Major says the man's a lunatic, and we shouldn't mess with him."

Man #2, "Suits me Ah weren't never big on takin a Reb. Prisoner, even when we were at war with them." He gets up, walks to the fire to check the bacon then picks up the coffee pot to pour himself a cup. There is a loud Boom and a ping as the coffee pot explodes. The man screeches in paine from the hot coffee. The others scramble to pick up their rifles and take cover.

Man #3 "Did he hit you Homer?"

"No, but he hit the coffee pot and the hot coffee burnt the piss out of me."

Man #1, "Did anyone see where the shot came from?"

Man #4, "Yea, I did. Look waaaaay up there on that ridge, you can still see the smoke trailin' away."

They all look up on a ridge

Man #2, "God damn. Are you sure? That's better than a half mile away, and he didn't miss by much."

Just then the skillet on the fire explodes.

The men all look at each other.

Man #2, "That coffee pot weren't no miss."

Man #1, "If he can shoot like that, five dollars a day ain't near enough. I'm gittin' the hell out of here. That Major's problem is his problem."

All four men pack up their gear, staying behind cover as much as they can. They all left riding in the direction of the main road.

On the ridge. Max smiles to himself, on the right side of his face.

Moments later in the Wilcox Mansion, the Major is in his bedroom in his dressing gown, coming out of a closet where there is a commode and a chamber pot. He carefully approaches a window. There he opens the curtain slightly to look out.

While he is looking out, a rifle muzzle touches the side of his head. He hears a double click of a rifle cocking. The Major, startled falls away from Max. Max continues to hold his rifle muzzle in the Major's face.

"Don't kill me. Don't kill me. I didn't have anything to do with what those men did to you. I didn't know anything about it until it was over with. I want you to know I reprimanded them severely for what they did."

"You reprimanded them?"

"Yes. Yes, I did. Especially Lt Garrett, he was the one that gave the order to do that.

"I know, I should have brought them up on charges, but the war was all but over, and they had served me so admirably all through it, I just couldn't bring myself to do that.

Max, sarcastically, "You didn't know anything about it until after it happened?"

"That's right, I didn't know anything about it; I was mortified when I found out. I swear it."

"You're a god damn liar Major." He hits the Major in the head with the gun barrel. "I saw you in your office window, watching the whole thing."

"No, no that couldn't have been me. It must have been someone else."

Max backs off a bit, and the Major gets up. He takes a quick peek out of the window.

"There ain't no one else in this entire creation with a beard as stupid lookin' as yours. You are lying Major. Do you know how many men there are that I hate worse than liars? .... Nine Major. The nine men that castrated me. You're one of them Major. You gave that order."

"No. Lt Garrett gave that order. Not me."

"Bullshit, Garrett was such a Lick-Finger, he wouldn't order a man to eat breakfast without your say-so.

74

The Major glances out the window.

"Speakin' of breakfast, if you're lookin for them fellers you hired to protect you, they left. Seems they don't like the vittles served around here."

"Don't kill me. I'll give you a lot of money to compensate you."

"You are going to give me money to compensate me?"

"I mean I am not admitting to any guilt, but you were woefully wronged, and it did happen within my command, so I feel a moral, (not legal) responsibility. I'll give you Just Compensation."

"Just what am I going to use that compensation for? Courtin' pretty women? To pay fancy whores? You see major that's something you don't seem to understand. What ya'll did to me can't be fixed. You left me without any kind of life to live for, yet still breathing. You see, that-there makes me a very dangerous feller. Nothing to live for, no fear of dying, and a big thirst for revenge, that's all Ah got to live for now."

"It may have been caused by a misinterpretation of an offhand comment, but I didn't give any of those orders, and you can't prove I did."

Max shakes his head, "you still don't understand. Ah don't have to prove nothin'. This ain't no court of law. All ah have to do is make up my mind. Ah'm the judge, jury and executioner. I'll find out, then Ah'll be back."

"You mean you ain't going to kill me?"

"Oh yea, Ah'm goin' to kill you. It's just, what Ah find will determine how Ah kill you. A head shot, or a belly shot. You better hope for the first one. I've seen men that got belly shot. It takes a long and painful time but you die anyway."

"But you aren't going to shoot me now?"

Max could see his mind working, likely on some kind of escape plan.

"Well, ah've changed my mind about that. All you've done is lie to me. Ah owe you some pain for that." Maxes' rifle fires two times hitting The Major's two knees. "

"Yea, and that will keep you from runnin' off."

The sun was just coming up over the pig farm. Rebecca was coming out of the back door of Mort Todd's clap-board shack. She is wearing an old ragged man's jacket as a robe. She had just gotten up and was heading to the outhouse. On a small stoop servicing the back door. there set a mason jar with four crocuses in water. She at first looked surprised then her expression turned to smile. She hurried to the outhouse to do her necessary things, then hurried back to start cooking a large breakfast. While the food was cooking, she was setting at her little, make-shift dresser, brushing her hair and humming. She is thinking that she has never been so excited about anything in her life. She also noted that the crocuses told her that Max was still alive and unhurt. She had been living with mixed emotions these last few days. On one hand she was so happy to have a man that she admired more than any man she had ever knew, and the thought that she might be able to share the rest of her life with him. On the other hand, there were men looking for him, some to kill him and others that would arrest him, and then kill him. Now that she had found him, she didn't know what she would do if she lost him.

She knew one thing; Now that she knows there is something so much better, she will not live the rest of her life with Mort Todd.

In the woods at the clearing, that he thought of as their place, Max was sitting on a large fallen tree, When he hears footsteps he ducked behind the log.

He heard Rebecca's voice, "Hello......Hello Max."

Max stands up and says, "Over here Becca. By the tree."

Rebecca rushes to him, sets the tray down and kisses him full on the mouth. She says, "Lordy Max Ah missed you so much. Ah know we ain't knowed each other but a short time, but ah just can't help thinkin' about you all the time, and worryin' about you something fierce

"I have been doing what you said, deciding if Ah wanted to go off with you. Yes! If you'll take me. There ain't no pondering' about it'; Ah do! And Ah hope you do.

"Ah've thought on it all the time too. It's strange how one hour can change a person's outlook on everything for the rest of his life. The truth is Ah want that too. Ah think, more than anything Ah ever wanted in my whole lifetime.

"Go on ahead and eat before it gets cold. We can still talk."

Between bites Max says, "Ah thought about you when Ah saw them crocuses because you said you liked them, and because They are like you. They're such hardy and pretty little flowers. Ah have seen them poke their yellow peddles up through the snow in freezing weather because they are wantin' so bad to get a little sunshine. And they deserve that sunshine."

"Are you sure you want to go with me. You know Ah can't pleasure a woman. After Mort's dead, they'll be lots of healthy, good fellers commin' around wanting court you, as pretty as you are. You might can have a normal life with them."

"Max!"

"You are pretty Becca. About the prettiest woman Ah have ever met."

"But Ah couldn't give them young'uns. Oh there would be lots of men coming around wantin' me to pleasure them but they would only wantin' to be bedding me not wedding me.

"No, it's you that ah want to be with. Ah don't care much about pleasurin' We can try some things in bed and if you like them, Ah'll do them for you, If you don't like them, we won't do them. And that will be OK.

"Ah'll be anything you want me to be to you. Ah'll be your girlfriend, your wife, or your whore. Anything, so long as I can be with you. Ah know it happened fast, but I love you more than anything.

"Do you think you could wake up to a face like mine every morning?"

"It's like that mirror and brush set Ah told you of. Ah don't love it for what it used to be, Ah love it for what it is now, and because it is mine and it always makes me feel good."

She walks to Max He put the tray on the fallen tree trunk. She takes his hands and coaxed him into standing up. She kisses him softly on the lips.

"To me Max, you are as beautiful as brand new."

"Alright. When Ah finish here Ah will take you with me, if you are still of a mind to go. Ah'll want you to be the first two things you said you'd be, but not the third."

She gives him an impish smile and says, "We'll see about that."

Max smiles at that, But then he gets sober, "You say you love me, and Ah believe you, but what if you get those special feelings, and ah can't do anything about them. That could put you into a powerful torment."

"First off Ah told you Ah growed up around four brothers. Ah reckon Ah've heard just about everything. Those special feelings are called Horney or Randy, And 'That Thing is called Fuckin'. We do have some things we gotta work out, and Ah think the only way that will happen is if we talk straight to one-another. The other day when Ah kissed you Ah felt your 'Little Max' start to get bigger. Does it ever get 'Proud'?"

"Sometimes."

"Have you ever tried doing it in your hand?"

"Good God Becca you're scaring me. Of course, Ah ain't never done that. That'll make a man crazy.

"No, it won't, that's an old wives-tale. If that would make a man crazy all my brothers would be crazy as loons, and they ain't........Well one of them is stupid but he ain't crazy."

"Well Ah ain't never done that." His face shows he is lying. Ah did try it with a 'Fancy Lady' after ah had healed up. All Ah got for mah trouble was laughed at."

'Max, all you need to satisfy a woman is to get hard down there. As a matter of fact, there are ways you could satisfy a woman even if you didn't have a little Max."

"Really?"

"Ah can show you those things so that ain't the problem. The problem is satisfying you. And Max, Ah would never laugh at you, about this or anything else, no matter what. She must have been a horrible person."

"Truth told, Ah never seen her laugh. But ah always felt that she did after Ah left. Bein' castrated ah ain't gonna need no satisfyin'."

"Ah reckon we need to think on that. Ah been raised around hogs all mah life. Ah know that a cut bore still gets horny. He'll try to poke a sow that's in season whenever he can."

Max thought for a while, "you know something just occurred to me. Ah've heard tell of them racehorse fellers puttin' a gelding in a pen with a mare that's coming in heat, cause the stud will try to mount her when she is just close, and the mare will kick the fire out of him until she is ready. Then when she accepts the gelding, they pull him off her and put the racehorse stud in and she lets him do his business. They do that so the mare don't injure the high dollar race-horse stud. That does show that a cut horse gets randy. Ah remember that because Ah always thought that was a dirty trick to play on the Gelding."

"That just proves what Ah was thinkin'."

"Yea, Ah do get big sometimes. Sometime Ah stay big for a long time, and if a cut horse and a cut bore get randy maybe Ah can. Ah don't know if ah could ever.....you know, finish?"

Becca looks at him. She stands up and begins unbuttoning her dress. She says, "Well, we are fixin to find out."

Twenty minutes later Max and Becca are lying in the leaves from last fall. The leaves made a crunching noise when they moved, and were a little scratchy on their naked bodies, but they did not seem to mind nor even notice. Becca sits up and starts putting her blouse on. She is smiling. Max is lying on his back watching her, he to, is smiling.

Max speaks, "Ah didn't think Ah could ever do that no more."

"That's the first time Ah ever enjoyed it, in my whole life-time. Now Ah kinda see what the fuss was all about. Ah used to do it to myself, and it was pleasant, but this was better than Ah ever imagined it could be.

"You used to do it to yourself? Really?"

"Yes. My brothers used to do it and they seemed to like it, so Ah tried it. It was good, but nothin' like this."

Max says, sheepishly, "Truth told, Ah have too."

"Ah think what we found out is, castratin' don't stop you from doing it completely. Maybe some tryin' this, and tryin' that, we can have a lot more pleasurin' than either of us thought."

"Maybe it just makes a man want to do it less."

'If that ever happens Ah'll be able to handle it.

"We can do it as much or as little as you want too. But one thing Ah did learn from Mort Todd is how to pleasure a man."

"Well now Ah have to think of a way to kill him two times. then.

"You, always remember, no matter how much or how little you want to do that, Ah will never think you any less of a man because of it. A man's what is inside you, not what comes out of your pecker."

"Well Becca, this has been so wonderful, but this changes things completely."

"How's that?"

"Ah care about if Ah get killed now. Ah didn't before."

"You just be a lot more careful then. Ah ain't fixin' to lose you."

Becca whispering, she puts her finger to her mouth. "Ah hear voices." She listens intently. "It's Mort and the Lt. and Ah think a couple of mah brothers. Oh God, the path they're on comes right through here."

Max looks around the clearing for something to hide behind. He jumps up, still naked, he runs to the horse. He strips the horse of his saddle with scabbard and bridle. He hides them behind a cedar tree and throws some leaves on them.

The men's voices are drawing closer. This is all he has time to do. He hides himself behind a cedar tree. He gets behind the tree just as the men ride into the clearing. Max spots his clothes and Henry rifle lying next to the fallen tree. He leans out from behind the cedar tree on the men's blind side, and hisses at Becca. She looks at him then quickly turns her head back and looks at Max out of the corner of her eye. He points to his rifle. She moves to where she drapes her skirt over the rifle. Becca is almost fully dressed. She notices Maxes' clothes lying

80

by the rifle, She scrapes them under her skirt as well, just as the men see her.

Becca hazards a quick look at Max. She sees his bare feet at the bottom of the tree. Using her hand hidden from the men she points at her feet and then at his feet.

Max looks at his feet then gets the message. He reaches down and carefully rakes some leaves over his feet and ankles. That didn't cover his legs completely but that was all he could do. The men were too close.

The five men ride into the clearing. Mort sees Becca sitting on the fallen tree trunk.

"Ro Becca what the hell are you doin' out here in the woods?"

"Zeke got out of his pasture-field, Ah had to come out here to git him.

"Damn woman, Can't you do anything? First Hector gits out, now Zeke's run off."

"It's hard, doin' all mah work and yours too. Ah found Zeke, he's just yonder. Ah'll bring him home when Ah come home. When are you coming home to stay?"

"When Ah kill that crazy som-bitch that's tryin' to kill me. Ah can't just stay home until he kills me! You, stupid bitch.

"You don't know what it's like to spend every minute wondering when a bullet's going to hit ya."

"Well, Ah'm sure tired of havin' to do everything by myself."

"Woman, when this is over me and you are going to settle some shit. Now git yer ass back to the house and fix us something to eat."

"Ya'll go on home. Ah'll be along in a few minutes. Ah got me some belly cramps, somthin' awful."

"You ain't knocked up are ya?"

"No Mort, it's just a woman thing. It'll be alright in a few minutes. "Ya'll go on." To her brothers, "Jed, are you and Bobby helpin' Mort now?"

"Hell no! He may be my brother-in-law, but Ah fixin' to git killed for him, that feller's good. Me and Bobby just met up with them back down the trail a piece."

Mort gives Jed a dark look.

"Ah told you Mort, That crazy man's your problem. Me and Bobby ain't gittin' involved in it.

The men leave. After the men are out of sight Becca breathes a sigh of relief. Max comes out of hiding, still naked. He takes Becca in his arms and kisses her. They look at each other and smile."

"Soon as they leave again come to the house and get Zeke. Ah don't want you to be without a horse.

"And Max. It ain't going to be as bad as we thought." She takes a good look at him and smiles.

Becca leaves. Max starts putting on his clothes.

CHAPTER TEN

At the Wilcox Mansion, in the middle of a large clearing.
Lt. Garrett, Todd and Moses ride toward the Great house.

Mort is saying, "Ah don't like this one damn bit. It's like we're ass-kissin' that fat som-bitch.

Garrett says, "We are not ass-kissing anyone. He says he has a plan for mutual protection, Is what his negra man said."

"Mutual protection my ass. The only ass he's worried about protectin' is his. Ah think we need to go find the Sheriff and make him take us into his posse. He can't refuse to let us ride with him. We're citizens."

"He didn't refuse to let us ride with him; He refused to let you ride with him."

"He's just doing that because he don't like me."

"I think he made that exceedingly clear when he said, 'I don't like you.' He said he don't trust you to take orders."

"Ah can take orders when ah agree with them."

"The fact remains, that the three of us just don't stand a chance against him and that rifle. It's just down to which one of us he decides to kill next."

"What do you suppose Wilcox has come up with?"

"I don't know, but I'm sure it will protect him more than it does us. Wilcox's nigra says he hired four men to protect him, but they skedaddled and right after that Max came right into the house and shot Wilcox in the knees. "

"See that's the thing, how can Wilcox be any help, layin' in bed all knee shot? Wonder why Trace didn't kill him when he had the chance?"

"I don't know. Trace has his own way of doing things. Well, let's see what Wilcox has to say. I certainly don't have any ideas. After we hear what he has to say we can decide if we want to do it or not."

The three men ride up to the front veranda. A portly woman comes to the door.

"Morning, Mrs. Wilcox. We're here to see your husband."

"Good morning Lieutenant." She looks down her nose at Todd. and didn't even acknowledge Moses. "The Major is expecting you, He is in bed because of the wounds that horrible man inflicted on him. He requested you be shown to his bedchamber.

Garrett's head snaps to the side. They hear a thunk of the bullet hitting Garrett's head, and a boom coming from the woods, then. Lt. Garrett falls dead on the veranda. Mrs. Wilcox screams. Todd and Fletcher take cover and start shooting in the direction of the smoke coming from the woods. Moses sticks his head up just enough to aim a shot when a bullet hits him in the forehead.

Mort panics. He draws his pistole and charges the smoke coming from the woods. He runs firing his pistol and screaming obscenities until it was empty. Mort stops but he continues to scream, and he continues to cock it and pull the trigger.

Max Grabs his Henry and fires into the ground just in front of Todd,

"Go ahead you Som-bitch kill me now if you're a mind to. Damn you. Ah'll see you in hell."

"That's likely, but it's not your time yet. It'll be soon though, Ah promise.

"Maybe Ah'll get you, you som-bitch."

"You know better than that Mort. You're scared, aren't you? Well, you should be, because Ah am going to kill you very soon.

"Bastard."

Max smiles his crooked smile and walks back into the woods to his horse.

Mrs. Wilcox shows Todd into Wilcox's bedroom. Having yet to greet him. It is dark because the drapes are closed. Wilcox is propped up with pillows. Candles are lit by the bed site to provide light.

Mort speaks first. "Well ah reckon it's down to just me and you. A'm sure you heard the shootion' out there. Garrett and Fletcher are both dead."

"Yes, my wife informed me.

"What kind of brilliant maneuver have you got to keep me and you alive? And how can you help, you can't do nothin' with your knees all shot up."

"I wish I could participate but I'm not even sure I'll ever walk again."

"Ah'm thinking you likely won't have to worry with that for very long. So, what's your fancy idea?"

"I want you to guard my home."

"Me? Buy myself?

"No. As you know, I hired four men to do that. That project failed miserably. However, I have found eight men that come very highly recommended."

"They'll just take your money and lay around on their asses. Till one of them gits shot, then they will all leave. They have no idea what they are up against."

"That is why I would put you in command of the endeavor. For which you will be paid handsomely. As will they."

"What are you paying them?"

"Each of you will receive twenty dollars a day and if you kill Trace each of you will receive one hundred dollars. While you men are here you can live in my barn and my cook will provide meals for you."

Mort thought for a moment. "Ah'll do it but, Ah want twice that and when we kill Trace Ah want five-hundred dollars.

"My God! That's a ridiculous amount of money."

"Yea, but Ah'm the one out there riskin' my ass much more than them. He might kill one of them if they git in his way, but me, he's out to kill me. So Ah'm taking more risk than anyone. And, Ah'll live in your guest room, not the barn.

"Oh no, my wife would never tolerate that."

"You just tell her to tolerate that, because that's the deal, take it or not."

"Alright."

"You were going to put the Lieutenant in charge, weren't you?"

"Oh no, I planned to put you both in charge."

"You are a liar. But ah guess we are stuck with each other, for now."

Mort went out to the barn. He is standing in front of eight men. They were tough looking men, all well-armed. Wilcox had informed them that Mort would be the boss.

Mort says, "Ya'll men have been in the Army so ya'll know the drill. Ah want four of you to man those barricades. One on each side of the house. There is only one of him so if one of you start shootin' Ah want all of you to come to that side. Four men will ride in the woods. Stay together! Stay in the woods. He won't get close, as he needs to be in the woods, to take on four men, but out in the open he'll shoot you from as far as that ridge way over yonder.

"Ah'll change you off, ever now and again."

Man #1; "Bullshit. Ain't no man could hit a body from that far off."

"Ah know seven dead men that would call you a liar. You keep cover or he will kill you. And, from that ridge. Or further."

From the ridge overlooking the Wilcox mansion Max is watching Todd and the hired men, through his telescope. He watches as four of the men take cover behind the makeshift works on each side of the house. He sees the other four men mount and ride into the woods as a group. He watches as Mort takes his bedroll into the house.

Max smiles, nods slightly. Puts the telescope away and mounts old Zeke and rides away into the woods. Now he knows where Todd will be for a while. He also knows where Becca will be.

Two days later a carriage pulls up in front of the house. Just as it gets to the house, flour shots sound from the inside.

Inside the carriage the Senator Wilcox ducks down. Mrs. Wilcox appears at the door.

"It's alright Senator, the shots can't reach you out here. I'm so glad you are home Senator. I'm at my wit's end Sir. I just don't know what to do."

The Senator sits up and cautiously exits the carriage. "What in the hell is going on here Emma? Who's doing all that shooting?"

"Winfield, Senator. He's been doing that all morning. "

"My God, what's that buffoon up to now?"

Mrs. Wilcox crying, "He's gone completely mad, Sir. He's in his bedchamber. He thinks he sees that man coming through the walls to kill him. He's shooting at him."

Todd comes out of the house.

The Senator says, "Who the hell are you and what are you doing here?

Ah was in the Major's Company B. He hired me to boss them guards. Mrs. Wilcox told me to come to the house when he started shootin'. Ah been tryin' to count the shots. Near as Ah can make out, he's shot about twenty-eight times. "

"Good Lord, how much ammunition does he have?"

Ah ain't sure exact. Before he went looney, he told me to bring him all the .32 ammunition for those two little Top Break Smith and Wesson pistols of his. That's two boxes."

"How many to a box?"

"Two boxes is forty bullets. So, then if he had likely six in each one, near as ah can figure he has eighteen shots left. "

Mrs. Wilcox says, "Senator, what ever are we going to do?"

"Well I am going to wait until he runs out of bullets. You can do as you wish. Forty rounds in the boxes, twenty-eight shots fired, and twelve rounds in his pistols, I'd think twenty-four left. All we have to do is count.

"Emma, the kitchen will be safe. See to some lunch. I'm hungry."

"But Senator, what are we going to do about Winford? I mean after he runs out of bullets?"

"Take him to the Asylum in Louisville. If he gets better, bring him home. If he does not, we will leave him there.

"And give word to the press that there was lunacy in his mother's family.

"Now, what do you have for lunch."

That afternoon they put Winford into a carriage. Bound and gagged, and Emma Wilcox getting in with a carpetbag.

The Senator instructs the negro hired hand, "Take the Major and Emma to the Asylum in Bowling Green."

Then to Todd, and the other men. "You men are no longer employed. When you get that mess cleaned up from around the house, I will pay you for the days worked, then I want you gone."

Todd and the men put the protective works away, then they all leave. Todd in one direction and the eight men in the other.

That afternoon Max and Becca are standing in the woods just a little way from the Todd cabin. Zeke is standing nearby.

Rebecca asks, "When is it going to be over, Max?"

"Soon. After Ah kill Mort and the Major, but they are the ones that deserve it the most."

"Ah wish you could stop now. Ah'm afraid for you."

Ah wish Ah could Becca, but then you would never be rid of Mort, and Ah wouldn't be true to the vow I made."

"Ah'm glad you ain't goin' to kill Owen Cheatham, and that Gray boy. Ah liked Owen, Ah didn't know Gray, but if Owen likes him, he's probably a good man."

"Maybe if Ah'd known all the facts, there's a couple more Ah wouldn't have killed. So, where's the heads and where's the tails of it."

"Maybe the tail's with Mort and that Major Wilcox."

88

"Ah hope. Truth told, Ah'm gitten' pure tuckered of it."

"Ah worried about Mort comin' home. He'll beat me now for sure, with Hector still gone, and Zeke missin'. Ah've kept the pigs fed, but Ah ain't done much else. Ah hope you get Mort before he git's home. Are you sure Mort's at that Wilcox plantation?"

"Yea, he's got a job there. He can't leave. Ah've just got to figure a way to git him alone, away from them other eight men. Ah don't want to kill them."

"Well, since he's there and we're here, do you want to ....Do it again?"

"Ah just ain't sure Ah can git those feelings again so soon."

"You just let me take care of that. Ah bet Ah can give you those feelings." Her hand reaches down into the front of his pants.

Fifteen minutes later they are lying naked on a bed of leaves.

"Ah reckon you won."

"Won what?"

"That bet. You won the bet."

"And Ah intend to keep on winnin."

Max smiles at her and they kiss.

The next morning finds Max lying on the ground looking at the Wilcox house and grounds. He finds the barricades are gone. He can find no evidence of the guards or Todd. He checks everything again, still nothing. He is puzzled and beginning to get worried.

An hour later Max is riding on the driveway to the Cheatham farm. His Henry in his right hand. He calls to the barn. "Cheatham, Max Trace, Ah want to talk to you."

Owen and Gray exit the barn carrying their long arms.

Max holds his rifle in the air then puts it in his scabbard. Showing peaceful intent.

Cheatham and Grey lean their guns against the barn and walk toward Max.

"How are ya'll today? James, has your wife had that baby yet?"

"Yep, three days ago. Twelve-pound baby boy."

"How's your wife and the boy?"

"She's OK now. Had a rough time of it, but Mary-Sue's takin' good car of her, says Jinny will be good in another day or so. She's still in bed but the baby's fine."

"Congratulations."

Owen says, "I'm sure you didn't come by here to pass the time of day. I heard you got Lt. Garrett and Fletcher. Garrett wasn't the worst of the lot. He just didn't have no balls at all. Always kissing Wilcox's ass. Mort going to be the last one?"

Mort and Wilcox, Ah still haven't killed him yet."

"You're going to have a hell of a time getting Wilcox."

"Max looks puzzled, "Meaning?"

"Oh. You ain't heard. Wilcox is on his way to Bowling Green to the Lunatic Asylum. Mort says he's gone crazy as a Whore-house bed-bug."

James says, "He started shooting up his bedroom, sayin' he saw you coming through the wall. Sayin' you were after him with a knife in one hand and your balls in the other."

Max thinks. "They sure he's crazy? He might just be fakin' it."

He shot nearly sixty holes in the walls and the ceiling, then started yellin' for Mort to bring him more ammo."

"Ah wish ah could say ah'm sorry to hear it but ah ain't. "

"You still going to kill him, Mr. Trace?"

"Ah don't reckon. Where he's at is worse than bein' dead. Ah'd be doin' him a favor. Which Ah ain't inclined to do."

"You say Mort told you that? When?"

"About half-hour ago. Mort said he spent the night in the 'Bottoms'

"Damn! Becca's home by her-self. "

"How do you know Becca?"

"Ah met her in the woods. Ah've got to go!"

Max turns Zeke and coxes him into the best gallop Zeke could manage.

Owen and James look at each other with perplexed expressions. Then Owen's eyes light up and a hint of a smile spreads across his face. He looks at James and says, "You reckon?"

James and shrugs, and grins.

Owen yells at Max, "He's been drinkin'. He's been to the 'Bottoms'. Hurry!"

CHAPTER ELEVEN

Max crouches behind the outhouse, His Henry rifle in his hand, watching through the open back door and listening to what was going on inside.

Todd was saying, "God damn woman can't you do nuthin, Ah told you to. Hector ain't back, Zeke's missing, Ah'll bet we got two or three sows that didn't git serviced."

"And Ah couldn't help that."

"That means we ain't gonna git no shoats. We can't run no pig farm without no shoats. You, dumb bitch."

"Ah couldn't git Hector to come home if Ah knew where he is."

"Ah told you to go git Jethro."

Ah told you why Ah don't want Jethro here when there ain't nobody else around. He keeps grabbin' ma tits and other intimate parts too. Don't you care if he does that?"

Well if he grabs your tits, Just slap the fire out of him. He knows if he was to fuck you, Ah'd beat him up real bad."

"Ah don't think you'd care, long as you git your precious hog back."

Todd starts taking his belt off. "You've bin sassin' me to much lately. Ah reckon Ah'm goin' to have to teach you better, again."

Max watches as he takes his belt off.

"Ain't no woman that belongs to me goin' to sass me."

Tod begins swinging and hitting Rebecca with his belt. Once across the back and once in the face. Max heads for the house on a dead run. As soon as he starts running, Todd's dogs start barking, alerting Todd.

Max grimaces at his mistake.

Todd hearing the dogs, Todd stops the beating and grabs his pistol and shoots. Max falls in the yard close to the house. Todd pounces on Max, putting the muzzle of his pistol at the base of Maxes' head.

"You just move, and Ah'll blow your brains all over this yard. EEEhhha. Ah got you, you som-bitch. You ain't gonna kill me. Ro-Becca, bring me a piece of rope from the slaughterin' tree yonder."

There is a large table under a huge oak tree, with a block and tackle hung over a large limb. There were two sturdy tables under the tree. It was the tables Todd used to slaughter and butcher pigs. There, is a large vat set up on bricks with ashes under it, next to the tables, for scalding the pigs to scrape the hair off. On one of the tables there was a wooden box that held knives, saws and cleavers, for butchering. There are several ropes and chains lying around the tables.

Becca looks at Maxes' face. His eyes are open, but there was blood on his face. Max looks at her and makes a quick nod toward the tree, indicating she should do as Tod said.

"Move your ass damn you. This is that mouther-fucker that was tryin' to kill me. Ah got his ass now!"

Becca is looking at Max's face. Max shifts his eyes toward the tree and nods. He doesn't want Todd to start back on Becca, not knowing how badly he is hurt and how much help he could be to her.

Becca moves toward the slaughterin' tree. She hands Todd the rope. Todd is tying Maxes hands behind his back.

Todd jerks max to his feet and drags him to the pullies at the tree. There he takes one of the ropes and ties it around Max's neck and ties it to the hook on the pully. He tightens the pully pulling Max on to his tip toes. And ties it off to the tree. Rebecca sees Max's wound is in his left side.

Todd says, "Well, mister tough man sharpshooter, Ah reckon Ah should have done a better job back in 'Hell's Gate'. Ah should Have cut your pecker off too. Ah reckon ah can finish that job now. For all you put me through this last month quick-killin' is too good for you."

Todd removes the oilskin from the box and removes a rusty knife.

Rebecca spots Max's Henry rifle lying on the ground near the tree.

Todd says, "last time ah took your man-seeds, this time Ah'll take it all.

"Well, mister tough guy you got the rest of them, but you didn't have the balls to get me." He found that exceptionally funny. Maybe ah didn't git your grit but Ah did get your manhood didn't Ah?" He was grinning.

"No you didn't!"

Tod turns to look at Rebecca. She was standing there with Max's Henry rifle, pointed at Todd's belly.

"What's wrong with you, you looney bitch? Put that God-damn rifle down or Ah'll beat you to death with it."

No, you won't Mort, You won't never beat me again, ever!"

"You mean you are siding with him over me? You may not know it, but he's the crazy bastard that' been tryin' to kill me. Ah'm your husband, you don't even know him."

Ah know real well who he is. Ah wanted him to kill you a long time ago, but he said he wanted to kill you last.

Todd went crazy, wild with anger. "You God damn fuckin' cunt!"

Todd lunges at Rebecca with the knife. Rebecca panics and fires the rifle. It was wild, but it grazes his head, and he falls on his stomach in the yard. Todd feels the crease in his head from the bullet. It was bleeding profusely. Blood coming down between his fingers.

Rebecca runs to Max. she lays his rifle on a table and grabs a knife from the box. She is cuts the rope attached to Max's neck.

94

Todd, realizing he was not hurt too badly, gets up and starts running at Max. Rebecca is working furiously with the dull knife, cutting the rope holding Max's hands. Just as Todd hits Max in the stomach with his shoulder, The rope parted releasing Max's hands. They both go down. Todd on top of Max.

Todd brings his knee up into Max's crotch. A blow that would completely disable a man with testicles, however Max felt very little pain from it.

They roll around hitting, kicking, biting. gouging. Until Max gets into a position where he could bring his knee into Todd's crotch. This totally paralyzes Todd, just as Todd hits Max's head with a rock, stunning him. Todd rolls off Max, He rolls against the tree holding his crotch. Max can't get up. He is dazed by the rock. Todd is recuperating, trying to get up.

Suddenly another shot rings out.

Todd is hit solid in the chest, causing him to fall back against the tree.

Max's eyes finally, focuses on Rebecca. She is standing there with the Henry rifle laboriously levering another round into the chamber.

Using every bit of effort and will power he could muster, Max stands up, just as Rebecca gets the rifle reloaded, Max comes to her side, he gently takes the rifle from her. Max says, "He's done for Becca. He'll never survive that heart shot."

Rebecca slumps into Max's arms. Max watching Mort.

Todd looks at his chest. He touches the blood then looks at Rebecca. "Ro-Becca, Damn you, Why?"

"You won't live long enough for me to tell you all the reasons, Mort. But mostly to keep you from killin' Max and to pay you back for my baby."

"Todd his voice halting, "You   and Trace?   How long?"

"About a week. He saved my life, Hector was attackin' me. He would have killed me, but Max stepped in front of me and shot him."

To Max, "You shot Hector? You, murdering bastard."

"Yea, that's what Ah do Todd. Ah murder people, See?"

He pulled his hair off his forehead, showing the scare from the branding.

"Ah was going to ask if the Major gave the order to castrate me. But ah reckon it don't matter no more."

"Yes, he gave that order, Kill that som-bitch."

"No Ah won't. Where he's at is worse than being dead. If he ever gets out, that'll be a nother matter."

"For now, Becca and me are going to make us a life together."

He laughs, causing him to cough, "Jokes on you Ro-Becca. He can't screw a woman."

"Yes, he can, and he has. He has satisfied me more this last week than you ever did in all the years we was married. Ah hated it with you."

"Slut.   Won't last.

"Maybe, but until then, Ah'll give him anything he wants for as long as he wants it. Ah hated some of those things you made me do, but Ah'll do them for him and be glad to if it pleasures him. Ah love Max." He's the best man Ah ever met."

"If he's so much man, why didn't you let us fight?"

"Bullyin' and beatin' men up that are smaller than you? IS that what you think bein' a man is? Ah never noticed you pickin' no fights with Gabe Bixby. Gabe would of whupped your ass all over town. No siree. You only picked on men smaller than you and women. You ain't no man a'tall."

"She   can't   give   you no young'un's."

"Neither can Ah. Remember? Yea, she told me you killed her baby.

"She   caused   it.

"You hit her and made her fall on her baby. How's that HER fault?

"She   wouldn't   do   what   Ah   told her."

"When Dr. Price told me ah couldn't pleasure him until after the baby come, he was tryin' to make me do it with my mouth, like them girls down in 'The Bottoms'. When Ah wouldn't do it, he hit me in the face. Knocking me off the bed on my baby, that was in my belly."

"Ah took   you   to the doctor."

"Yea, after you made me do what you wanted, but then it was too late. The Doctor said Ah had lost too much blood. Ah almost died, myself. Ah want you to know Mort, Ah hate your guts."

Max looks at Todd. He walks over and pulls an eyelid open. "He's dead, Becca.

"Ah wanted him to know."

"Ah reckon he knew."

Rebecca looks at Mort. Neither remorse nor joy, just the conclusion to a trying chapter of her life. She nods her head once.

With the knife she cuts a piece of her petticoat and bandages Maxes' wound. Tight so as to stop the bleeding.

CHAPTER TWELVE

O wen Cheatham is eating his supper when he hears his dogs barking. He looks out the front window to see Sheriff Barton and five men riding up his driveway toward the house. Owen walks out into the front yard and greets the men.

"Morning Sheriff, gents."

The sheriff nods to Owen, "Morning Owen. I'm on my way to Mort Todd's place. I'm told he's been done to death.

Owen nods, "It figures."

"You don't seem surprised.

"Ah'm not. I knew it was coming. That should be an end to it though."

"He's another one that was in ya'll's Army Company, isn't he?"

"Yea."

"What about you?"

"He ain't going to kill me."

"You know what this is all about don't you?"

"Yes."

"I want you to ride with me to Todd's, and on the way, you can tell me what the hell is going on."

"I'll saddle my horse."

"I talked to Wilcox before he went nuts but trying to get the truth out of him is like trying to milk a rock."

On the ride to the Todd farm, Owen filled Sheriff Barton in on the full story.

"Good God! They castrated, him? And you say Wilcox ordered it? Ain't no wonder he's killing people. So, you don't think he will kill any more men?

"I don't think so. He told me at the beginning of this thing, that he wasn't going to kill me. He told James Grey that he took him off the list, and what with Wilcox going loony, he said, that was better than him being dead. He said that if Wilcox got well, he might rethink that.

"Do you believe him?"

"Yea. He puts store in his word,"

"Sounds like you admire this man."

"Some. He has an honesty about him that I admire. Has so far as I have known him."

"Whatever his motivation, he has killed eight men in my county. I need to see him hang.

"I don't agree with all he did. Some of those men he killed were good men that just thought they had to follow orders, no matter what they were."

"Do you know where this trace fellow hails from?"

Owen shakes his head, "Don't know. Seems like I heard something about Tennessee, but I ain't certain."

Sheriff Barton thinks for a moment. "If he pulls foot for parts unknown, I am going to be left holding the shitty end of the horn. He's got the whole county in an uproar, especially the Senator. He's calling for my scalp."

"Well, you had yourself a mighty tough job, Sheriff."

"Cheatham, If I tell the story you told me to the Cox County Courier, will you back it?"

"Yes, I'll tell it to them myself. It's the truth."

"Will James Gray affirm it?"

"Yes. He'll tell the truth. I just want to make it clear that James and some of the others thought they <u>had</u> to do what they did."

The Sheriff nods.

At the Todd pig farm, four men walk out to meet the posse. One elderly fat man and three younger men. (Rebecca's father and brothers)

Rebecca's father says, "You gotta find that murderin' bastard, Sheriff! He killed Mort, and kidnapped my Becca, and took a bunch of stuff. No tellin' what he's doin' to her."

The sheriff looks at Owen. Owen looks skeptical and shakes his head.

"What did he steal?"

"He took a bunch of her clothes, he took a hairbrush set her momma gave her just before she died, and some purty dishes that were her momma's. And some furniture. Nice stuff handed down from my Carrie's maw. Took Mort's wagon and horse, too."

"Where's Mort's body?"

"Out back by the saughterin' tree."

The men dismount and walk around the house to Mort's body lying at the bottom of the big tree.

"Has any of you touched the body?"

Son #3 says, "No sir! It's bad luck to touch a dead man. That's bad luck."

The Sheriff looks at him with a frown. "Must be hell on morticians and Doctors.   And Sheriffs too."

The Sheriff touches Mort's face. He lifts his arm and let it go. It flops back down. "Body's still warm and not stiff yet. Must have been dead only a few hours. His neck is just starting to get stiff. He has a bullet crease on the top of his head. One in the chest. Looks like this was a gun fight."

The sheriff goes through Mort's pockets. He finds a gold watch, 23 dollars and change, a rabbet's foot and a plug of chewing tobacco. He puts it all in a bag, except the tobacco, which he put in his pocket.

Owen looks at him and smiles.

"It's my brand.

"If he's from Tennessee then that's where he's headed. Arnold, Come here." One of the posse comes to him. "He likely headed to Tennessee. Take the rest of the posse and ride as fast as you can down the Gallatin road. That the fastest way to Tennessee. Try to ketch him but be very careful. Remember that man is dangerous, as hell."

"You ain't coming?"

Soon as I finish here. I'll follow you soon as I can."

The posse leaves at a gallop.

Sheriff Barton goes through the house, picking through things, writing in a notebook. He finds Todd's Spencer rifle sitting by the bed.

The sheriff and Owen exchange looks.

Owen says, "Don't look like a kidnapping or robbery to me. This morning when I told Trace that Mort had left my place going home, He said, 'Oh my God! Becca's home by herself.' Now, he called her Becca, not Rebecca or Mrs. Todd, and he looked panicked."

"Do you think there is something going on between Trace and Rebecca Todd?"

Owen nods, "I saw Trace beaten and tortured more than you can believe. I never saw fear in his face until today. That fear was for Becca."

"Sounds like you are right, but I would hate to put that into a formal report, without more proof."

Owen nods, "He didn't take Mort's gold watch, or the money in his pocket."

"He took her clothes."

"Right."

"And I have seen Becca's wardrobe, All of it would wouldn't bring two dollars at a rummage sale. And if he let her take the things precious to her......."

The Sheriff nods, "From talking to her brothers none of it was of any account."

"Unless, they were given to you by a loved one."

"Your likely right. But, if he's done killing and left the state, I'd better start looking for a new way to make a living. If I don't catch him, my odds of getting re-elected aren't a lot better than winning the Kentucky Derby race riding a jackass.

"Oh well, I hear Bixby's Blacksmith Shop is For Sale."

"If we get the whole story put in the Courier, maybe it might take some of the pressure off you. A lot of men will see his side of it."

"I hope you're right, but that doesn't even address how much I'm over budget for the posse all month. Nobody likes that, but if I catch him, they might forgive it."

The posse riding at full gallop, catches up with Max and Becca at a pass between two steep hills. Max stops the wagon, turning it at about forty-five-degree angle to the road. Max retrieves his Henry rifle from the saddle scabbard in the back of the wagon. They stop just past the sign saying "YOU ARE NOW ENTERING THE STATE OF TENESSEE

Max fires a few rounds over the heads of the posse, causing them to stop and take cover. He and Rebecca take cover behind the wagon. Rebecca has her arm around Max.

Arnold says, to the posse, in a loud voice, "Stop shooting. The girl's too close. If we hit her, the Sheriff will skin us."

Max sneaks along the side of the wagon. He reaches over the side of the wagon bed and gets the Whitworth rifle, the telescope sight and his 'Possibles' bag.

He tells Rebeca, "You stay here. They won't hurt you. Tell them Ah made you come with me."

Rebecca takes a long look at him. She nods, but the look on her face showed she didn't intend to comply."

Max starts hobbling to the trail through the woods, carrying both rifles. Moving slow because of his bad leg and the wound in his side. He was expecting fire from the posse, there was none. Max ventures a look at the posse. He sees Rebecca running along his side shielding him from the posse.

They reach the woods, no shots fired.

"Damn Becca, ah told you to stay with the wagon."

"If Ah had they would'a shot you. You said yourself they wouldn't hurt me. And besides Ah'm in this with you 'for better or worse.'

They make it twenty yards, about halfway up the hill, there was a large rock they could use as cover, with a good command of the path. The path was the only way the hill could be climbed.

Rebecca looks at the wound in Maxes' side. it was starting to bleed again. She tightens the bandage she had put on the wound.

Arnold says, "Take cover. Ya'll have seen what he can with that rifle. I don't think he can go any higher up that hill, it's too steep, Ben, see if you can get to your horse. If you can, ride back to the Sheriff and tell him we have him trapped."

Max tells Rebecca, "This is it Becca, I'll have good cover. They will have a real hard time tryin' to come up through the woods. Ah hope they don't try. Ah can hold them off from here."

"You mean, we."

Becca maybe it's right for me to die on this hill. Ah killed a lot of men, some Ah found out were good men. You didn't hurt nobody."

"Except Mort. Ah'm stayin' Max."

"No. Go on back down. Tell them Ah forced you. They think Ah killed Mort. If Ah can git away Ah'll come for you after a while. If not, you'll find yourself a good man someday. Even if we could get away all the things you love are in that wagon."

"No Max the thing Ah love the most is right here next to me. Ah don't know what our fate is going to be, but we are goin' to share it.

On the road about a mile from the confrontation, Posse member Ben meets with Owen and the Sheriff, riding at a trot. Ben tells them of the situation, "We got them, but it's a 'Mexican Standoff'. He's on a hill that leads to a bluff, but if we try to go up that hill, he'll be able to pick us off all day long."

When they reach the standoff site, the Sheriff looks the situation over. To Owen, "Ben's right, We have him boxed, but now what the hell are we going to do with him?

Arnold heard, "WE tried to climb up on both sides, through the woods and flank him. He shot Kent in the leg, and almost took Braxton's head off. Shot a hole in his hat.

The Sheriff looks at Owen. Owen shakes his head. "If he was shooting at Braxton's head, Braxton would be dead. He shot at Braxton's hat. He's tryin' not to kill any of your men, Sheriff."

Sheriff Benton nods his head in agreement. "Would he respect a white flag?"

"Ask him. If he says he will then, he will."

The Sheriff yells up the hill, taking a white handkerchief from his pocket. "Trace. If I come up under a white flag will you honor it?"

"Yes. Come up with no guns."

The Sheriff climes the hill until he gets to about ten-yards from the rocks."

"That's far enough Sheriff. Is Cheatham in your posse?

"No. I tried to deputize him, but he said no. He said he gave you his word, he wouldn't ride against you, and he won't break his word. He is just observing."

"Ah'm glad to hear that. I kinda like him. What do you want?"

"I want you to surrender. I will promise you a fair trial. When folks hear what they did to you, I think you might just get off. I noticed you ain't hurt nobody but the ones that did that to you."

"By the book It's still murder. And then Wilcox's daddy being a Senator,   No. I'd rather die here on this hill than to hang or spend the rest of my life in a prison."

"Well turn the girl lose. Ain't no call for her to get hurt."

"No. He aint holdin' me against my will. He tried to make me go, but ah'm gonna stay with him, what-ever happens."

The sheriff says to himself, "Well, there goes my kidnapping charge."

"Ya'll might git me, but Ah got good cover and Ah'll get most of you first. Ah've got no call to kill your men, or you Sheriff. Ah got no bone to pick with you or them. If you send them up here to kill me, Ah'll kill them."

104

"Well that's it then. Rebecca come on down. I won't charge you with nothing, but if you start shooting, I will have to. "

"No. You're going to have to kill me too, Sheriff."

Sheriff Benton comes back down the hill. He walks to his horse. Takes a drink from his canteen. He bites off a chew of tobacco and looks up the hill shaking his head. He checks his rifle load.

He is obviously agonizing over his decision. He looks at the sign in the ground just to the side of the road. He walks to his posse and drops a bombshell. "Get your gear men. We're going home."

The men and Owen get shocked expressions on their faces.

"We're in Tennessee. Out of our jurisdiction. Didn't ya'll see that sign about ten-yards back?"

Arnold says, "After eight murders, ain't nobody going to nit-pick that."

"We're pulling out."

Arnold says, What about the wagon?"

"That's my wagon and my stuff. If you take It ya'll are stealin'."

The Sheriff laughing. "Leave it." He walks to where Owen is standing with the horses, "Have you got any blacksmith work you need done?"

"When I do, you'll get it."

CHAPTER 13

SPRING 1869 Hendersonville Tenn.

On a spring afternoon about three-years later. At a farmhouse in Sumpter County Tennessee a lone rider comes riding in from the road on the farm's driveway. A few dogs bark.

Max and Rebecca come out the front door of a well-kept farmhouse to see who it is.

Max is not wearing a patch over his eye. His carefully trimmed beard covered the misshapen jaw line. He wore his hair combed to swoop down over the 'M' scar. He looks normal, but still has a slight limp.

Max recognizes him. "Well, good afternoon Owen."

Rebecca says, "Owen! What in the world are you doing in Tennessee?"

"I'm here on business. Came to see a man in Gallatin about some Jersey Cows. James and I are running a dairy farm now."

"That would be Mr. Bright."

"Yes. I just happened to recall when you told Wilcox, 'If you want that rifle so bad, after the war, you come to Gallatin and I'll give it to you, one bullet at a time.'"

"Yea. Ah remember that."

"So, Ah asked Mr. Bright if he knew you, and he told me where your farm was. Don't worry, I aint here to wake snakes."

"If that's so, lite and have supper with us. It's good to see you again."

Inside the house parlor Rebecca and two girls can be seen in the kitchen preparing a meal. A small boy is playing in the yard.
'Owen nods puzzled, "The children?"
"Adopted. We wanted children, They need a maw and pa."
"I hope I ain't prying to much, but you look a sight better than you did when I saw you last. Even your eye."
'It's glass. A feller in Nashville makes them. Colors them to match."
"Even your jaw looks better, I can't even tell it, the beard covers it so well."
"Well Ah've got me a fine barber now." He looks at Rebecca and smiles. She winks at him.
Owen Sees the smile and nods his head, smiling."
In the kitchen Rebecca flips an errant sprig of hair, but it falls right back. She tells the girls, "Ah've got to fix this hair. Ah'll be right back."
Rebecca walks into a very nice bedroom. There, is a lovely carved oak dresser, with a big mirror attached. She picks up her hairbrush and hand mirror set. The paint is still chipped, but the mirror is no longer cracked, the brush bristles have been replaced. She repairs her hair and lays the set, gently back on her dresser, and smiles at it.
Back inside the parlor Owen notices the Whitworth rifle on pegs over the fireplace. He walks over and looks at it. "So, this here's the rifle that caused the whole thing. It certainly looks like a quality piece."
"That rifle didn't start it. Major Wilcox did, when he ordered me castrated."
"I reckon that's true, but the rifle was a big part of why he did it. Is it as accurate as they say?
"What the longest shot you ever made good with it?"

Max lifts the rifle off it's pegs and hands it to Owen. "Ah reckon the longest confirmed shot would be about Twelve-hundred yards. Some General at the battle of Spotsylvania."

"Oh my God. You're the one that got General Sedgewick? That shot is famous. Everyone was talking about it. Did you know that at the very time you shot him, He was riding back and forth chiding his men from ducking so much. He was telling them, "Not to bother ducking, no one could hit an elephant from that far away."

Ah never did know his name, but Ah killed a General there from that distance." Changing the subject. "Is Wilcox still in that Asylum?"

Owen nods, "Yes. They don't ever expect him to recover. Would you go back if he did?"

"Ah don't know. Ah would hate the thought of him living a good life, but now, Ah have a lot to lose."

"Did getting revenge make you happy?"

Max shakes his head, "Can't say. Just about the time Ah finished what Ah had to do, Ah met up with Becca, and Ah become a very happy man. One of them did it."

"I'd reckon, Becca."

"Oh yea. Ah reckon mostly it's Becca. Ah don't think there's another woman in the whole of this world that could of, or would of, showed me Ah can still be a man."

Owen is a little confused, "You mean you can still.........Ah...."

"Sometimes, but it takes a very special woman to bring it out. Becca's the best thing that ever happened to me. Ah love her more than Ah love livin'."

Owen looks around the room, pausing at a picture of Max. Becca and the children, sitting beside a mason jar full of crocus flowers.

"She sure seems happy. I'd say you were the best thing that ever happened to Becca too."

Max offers Owen his hand. They shake hands.

THE END.

This Novel is also written in Screenplay format. Maybe someday? Until then check for more from O.K. Williams @ *www.okwilliams.com*